DISNEY
TALES FROM
ADVENTURELAND

THE
KEYMASTER'S
QUEST

Written by Jason Lethcoe
Illustrations by Jeff Clark
Cover paint by Grace Lee

Printed in the United States of America
First Hardcover Edition, September 2017
1 3 5 7 9 10 8 6 4 2
FAC-008598-17223
Library of Congress Control Number: 2016938195
ISBN 978-1-4847-8143-2

For more Disney Press fun, visit www.disneybooks.com

DISNEY
TALES FROM

ADVENTURELAND

THE KEYMASTER'S QUEST

Jason Lethcoe

DISNEY PRESS

LOS ANGELES · NEW YORK

For Nancy, my greatest adventure.

Chapter One
Rest in Peace?

It wasn't an ordinary funeral. At least, Andy Stanley didn't *think* it was. True, Andy had never *been* to a funeral before, but he was fairly certain that there was usually a body . . . or a casket . . . or at least *some* evidence that the person in question was in fact *dead*.

Perhaps Andy shouldn't have been surprised. After all, his grandfather wasn't exactly conventional—or so Andy had been told. Andy had never so much as spoken to his grandfather, but he had heard plenty of stories about Ned Lostmore. He had practically memorized the legendary archaeologist's many books, with titles like *Carnivorous Plants I've Nearly Been Eaten By* and *Witch Doctors: A Prescription for Madness?*

Andy wondered why everyone was so ready to accept the worst and proclaim Ned gone. He knew little about the details surrounding his grandfather's disappearance other than the fact that he had been looking for a temple hidden deep in the Amazon jungle. The last communication anyone had received from Ned was a letter sent to the university where he worked, stating that he had found the temple and was determined to explore it. The temple was infamous for its protection spells. Legend claimed that any mortal who entered would never return.

Andy assumed that most people would have ignored those legends, brushing them off as nothing more than superstitious mumbo jumbo. But Ned Lostmore was different. Andy knew from reading his grandfather's books that Ned took such curses very seriously. He also knew how seriously his grandfather took his work. Andy guessed that the possibility of finding ancient artifacts inside the temple would have made Ned brave any danger. Not even the threat of hidden traps and deadly poisons would have deterred the intrepid jungle doctor from achieving his goal.

But no one knew what Ned had found. He had never returned from the temple, and a search of the area around his last known location had revealed no trace of him. It seemed that Ned Lostmore had simply vanished into thin air!

Now Andy found himself standing at the funeral of a grandfather he had never met, surrounded by the strangest assortment of people he had ever seen.

Andy had always felt self-conscious around people he didn't know. He tended to fidget and repeatedly smooth his blond hair, convinced that he looked strange and out of place. And in fact, Andy *did* look out of place in this crowd. Dressed in his best suit and tie, his hair only slightly ruffled, he was by far one of the most *normal* people in sight.

Andy was still taking in the strange collection of funeral attendants when a short man wearing an elaborate tribal mask and headdress approached him.

"Greetings, dear boy," the man said, reaching out to shake Andy's hand. "You must be Andy Stanley! Your grandfather described you perfectly. Dr. Cedric Willoughby Marcus Theodore Bunsen the third, at your service."

Andy shook the man's hand, at a loss for words.

The man's voice was crisp and clear, tinged with an English accent that would have made him seem quite proper if not for the ferocious mask covering his face. Andy tried to pull his eyes away from the mask, but he couldn't do it. *I wonder what his real face looks like*, he thought. *There must be a reason he wears a mask!*

"By jingle, look at that!" the doctor exclaimed suddenly.

"What?" Andy asked, finally finding his voice.

Cedric grabbed Andy's hand and studied his fingernails intently. Andy tried to pull away, but the doctor had a stronger grip than Andy would have expected from a man of his stature.

"You have a rare case of the Ogopogo River Jimmy-Jams!" the doctor said. He paused a moment to think and then asked, "Have you been petting any hippos lately?"

"Ummm . . . no," Andy said, puzzled. *Hippos? Is he crazy? Why would I pet a hippo?*

"Not to worry, my boy. I have just the thing!" the doctor said. He rummaged through a small pouch at his belt and produced a clay jar, which he shoved into Andy's hands. "Hold on to the contents inside when you sleep at night. You'll be cured within the year."

Andy stared down at the jar. He didn't know whether to thank the witch doctor or run away from him. Cedric was obviously off his rocker.

The doctor seemed to sense Andy's hesitation. He leaned over and whispered conspiratorially, "Don't worry, I studied at Cambridge. Inside the jar is a pair of giant crocodile teeth. Very magical."

Andy managed a small chuckle, but the doctor didn't seem to be joking. He just stared at Andy through the eyeholes of his mask.

Andy edged away from him, feeling uncomfortable. "I'd better see what my parents are up to. Um . . . thanks for the teeth."

"Don't mention it, dear boy," Cedric said. "Your grandfather specifically told me to watch out for you. I have plenty more cures where that one came from, should you ever have need of them."

"Right. Thanks . . ." Andy mumbled, backing toward the crowd of people gathered in the yard behind his grandfather's house.

He looked at the jar of teeth in his hand. *What do I do with these?* he wondered. Before he could come up with an answer, he heard someone call out, "You there!"

Andy's whole body stiffened. He turned to see a large barrel-chested man with a red handlebar mustache approaching him rapidly. Andy stood still, arms stiff at his sides. He was too afraid to do otherwise.

From a distance, the man looked relatively normal. But as he got closer, Andy saw that where his left eye should have been was a shiny steel ball. Andy stood up straighter, trying not to stare at the man's metal eye. But he couldn't keep his mind off it. *What is it with Grandfather's friends? First a tribal mask and now a metal eye? How does someone even lose an eye?* he wondered. *And why replace it with a piece of metal?*

The big man stared down at Andy. "What's your name, private?"

"Andy Stanley, sir," Andy replied. He hated the way his voice shook when he answered.

The man looked Andy up and down. "Stanley, did you say? *Andy* Stanley?"

Andy continued to stare forward as the big man lowered his head next to Andy's, peering closely at the boy's face with his one good eye. After a moment, he grunted. Then, to Andy's surprise, the man let out a big guffaw. "Ha! Had you going there, didn't I?" he said, laughing. "Nice to meet you. I'm Captain Rusty Bucketts, bush pilot and adventurer."

Andy relaxed and tried to smile. His stomach was still churning as he shook the big man's outstretched hand. The crushing grip that enfolded his own made Andy gasp with pain, but Rusty hardly seemed to notice.

"I recognized you at once. You look just like your grandfather," he said. "We flew over eighty missions together in the Great War. He's a great man, to be sure. Nobody can match the indomitable Ned Lostmore!"

Andy startled at hearing the pilot refer to his grandfather in present tense. But before he could give it another thought, Rusty whirled him to the left and introduced him to a pair of ladies.

"Betty, Dotty, allow me to introduce Ned's grandson, Andy Stanley."

Andy was taken aback. The beautiful ladies in front of him were conjoined at the hip! The two wore matching dresses, each black with a jade and silver dragon woven into it. They smiled at him, their dazzling white teeth gleaming. Both were rather tall and had glossy black hair and high cheekbones.

"Charmed," said the one Rusty had introduced as Betty.

"Absolutely charmed," said Dotty.

"The sisters are accomplished belly dancers. They've performed for heads of state across Europe and the Far East," Rusty said.

Andy didn't know what to say to that. His cheeks flushed with embarrassment and he stammered a reply.

"I . . . I'm sure you're quite good at it," was all that he could manage.

The sisters laughed, noticing how uncomfortable he was.

"We do more than dance," Betty said.

"Yes, we're *much* more than just dancers," Dotty said.

The women narrowed their eyes and grew serious. They leaned toward Andy and hissed in unison, "We're the best assassins your grandfather ever worked with. Don't let appearances deceive you, boy."

Andy's eyes widened and he nodded vigorously.

I certainly won't! he thought. The change that had come over the women had caught him completely off guard. It was like admiring a beautiful animal from afar only to get close and see its teeth dripping with venom— shocking and hard to reconcile in his mind.

Andy shook his head, processing the women's words. Why would his grandfather need to work with assassins?

He was trying to figure out what to say to the women when he heard the funeral director calling for everyone to gather around, his voice ringing out above the crowd. Relieved, Andy excused himself and rushed off to find his parents. He was moving through the crowd so quickly that he accidentally bumped into someone. He looked up to see a face covered with white makeup. The lips were painted a bright cherry red, and black makeup outlined the eyes.

A mime?

The girl looked at Andy and smiled broadly. Then she began to speak rather loudly and at a rapid pace.

"You must be Andy! I've known your grandfather for years! He and I met when I was in Paris. I had just learned how to act like I was trapped in an invisible box! Of course, I hadn't learned how to do it properly. Most people thought I was fighting off invisible mosquitoes. I tried to explain to everyone what I was doing, but only your grandfather guessed what I was really pretending to do. And of course, once he discovered that I was not only a mime but also an opera singer, he told me how much he loved the opera, too! We both love opera! Isn't that funny?

"I can't believe it's really you, Andy! Your grandfather said you might come, but I hardly expected . . . I mean, I knew that you probably *would* come, but you didn't know him, did you? And I wasn't sure you'd travel all the way to Oregon for a man you'd never met. I thought maybe you'd rather stay home, where it's safe, and read a book. But then, Ned always said that there was much more to you than it seemed at first glance. Not that there's anything wrong with you at first glance. You're a nice-looking boy. I actually thought you'd be shorter. My name's Molly, by the way. Say, have you combed your hair lately? It's sticking up in the front. Here, let me. . . ."

Molly reached into a pocket and whipped out a comb. Andy tried to back away, but she had a surprisingly strong hold on his arm and kept him firmly in place as she ran the comb through his cowlicks.

Andy sighed. It seemed he had no choice but to stay put until she was done. *What does she mean, home is safe?* he wondered. *Is it not safe here?*

Andy shook his head. Molly was still blathering on about something or other. "I, uh, thought mimes weren't supposed to talk," he said as she tugged on a particularly obstinate tangle. "Ow!"

Molly ignored him and just kept babbling. The more she talked, the more Andy wished for some of that famous mime silence he'd heard about.

"I think that you should stop reading about your grandfather's adventures and try having one of your own, you know? It's not healthy to stay inside reading so much. A boy your age needs fresh air, excitement. And it wouldn't hurt for you to get more protein in your diet. You're looking a bit paler this week than you did a couple of months ago. More meat and vegetables, young man, that's the secret."

Why is she acting like she knows me? Why are all of Grandfather's friends acting like they know me—like he knew me? I've never met the man, and I don't think Mom has spoken to him in years! Has Molly been watching me? Has he been watching me?

"There, that's better!" Molly finally said with a grin. She flipped her comb into the air and landed it expertly on top of her black beret. Andy didn't know whether to thank her or laugh. Luckily, he was saved from having to decide by the funeral director's announcement that the ceremony to honor his grandfather was about to begin.

"Ladies and gentlemen, please make way for Nicodemus Crumb," the funeral director called. "Step aside, now. Those metal rods he's carrying have sharpened tips, and we don't want anyone to get hurt."

Andy glanced up to see a strange-looking man in gray robes enter the yard with a handful of homemade lightning rods. The man's face was a web of deep wrinkles, and he limped when he walked. Looking closer, Andy noticed that this was because of a carved peg leg with strange symbols etched into it.

Ned's will had outlined specific instructions for the kind of ceremony to be performed upon his death. Apparently, this Nicodemus Crumb was the only one who could perform the appropriate rites. Once again, Andy couldn't help wondering how his grandfather had come into contact with such a man.

He sure knew some interesting people, Andy mused.

Nicodemus Crumb planted the iron poles in a circle around the crowd. At the center of the circle sat an easel holding a black-and-white photograph of Andy's grandfather. Then he asked everyone to join hands, forming a large ring between the photo and the lightning rods.

Andy gulped. Now he *knew* this was no ordinary funeral. But he had always been one to follow orders.

So with another deep breath, he set down the jar of crocodile teeth and, stepping forward, took the hands of the nearest people—one of the belly dancers and the mime.

Satisfied that a proper circle had been formed, Nicodemus began to shout in a high, raspy voice, *"Injunctae stormous lightinea!* We call upon the four winds to honor the passing of Nedley Lostmore! Let the earth mourn his passing and the clouds demonstrate their fury! *Injunctae stormous lightinea!"*

Andy could tell that a storm had been building all day. The air felt electrically charged, and a cool wind was already blowing from the south.

Whether Nicodemus Crumb actually knew how to summon the storm was debatable, but Andy knew that putting a bunch of tall metal rods in the middle of a flat yard was asking for trouble. Every fiber of his being demanded that he leave right then and there. The thought of being struck by lightning terrified him.

Andy tried to get his parents' attention to let them

know he wanted to leave. But try as he might, he couldn't subtly catch their eyes. He tried clearing his throat and coughing loudly, but his mother and father were so absorbed in the unusual ceremony that they didn't so much as glance at him.

Finally, in a fit of desperation, Andy tried to extricate himself from his place in the assembled circle and move to where his parents were standing.

And that was when his clumsiness kicked in.

Andy tried to be careful. He always tried! But like so many times before, his shoelace had come undone and he tripped over it. Andy's arms flailed wildly, and he grabbed for something to stop his fall. Unfortunately, the only thing nearby was one of the lightning rods. Andy's fist closed around the rod, but it wasn't strong enough to break his fall. As he hit the ground, the rod came free, flew from his hands, and conked Rusty—the pilot with the artificial eye—on the back of the head.

The force catapulted the pilot's steel eye through

the air and across the circle, where it smashed into Molly the mime's forehead. Molly let out a terrified yelp and stumbled into a massive torch, which fell over and ignited a patch of dry grass in the middle of the circle.

Andy watched in horror as the crowd released their clasped hands and raced forward to try to put out the fire. By the time they succeeded, Ned's picture had been burned to ashes.

Nicodemus, who had singed off his eyebrows while trying to rescue his lightning rods from the blaze, turned to face Andy.

Andy gulped. *This is not going to be good.*

So, trusting his earlier judgment, he turned and ran back to his grandfather's mansion, leaving the ugly scene behind.

Andy walked quickly through his grandfather's luxurious home, tugging desperately at his tie, eager to loosen it and breathe normally. What had just happened rattled his nerves, and he wanted to go somewhere quiet where he could think.

As he walked down the hallway toward his grandfather's study, Andy caught sight of his reflection in an ornate mirror hanging on the wall. He was pale and thin. His blond hair was once again sticking up in all directions from his running his hands through it, and his brown eyes were bloodshot. The trip to his grandfather's house had taken two days, and he looked in desperate need of a good night's sleep.

Andy made his way into the study and flopped down in a big leather chair by the fireplace. He felt something poke him in the back. Leaning forward, he reached into his pocket and tossed the contents onto the table in front of him. A key and a letter hit the table's surface with a loud thud.

A week before the funeral, Andy had received a strange package in the mail. Inside was a note from his grandfather's attorney informing him that his grandfather had left him an inheritance. Andy wondered what the man who had never cared enough to meet him could possibly have left for him. A book? An ancient artifact? Piles of money?

His initial excitement about the prospect of wealth had evaporated when he arrived at his grandfather's mansion and learned that the inheritance was no more than an ornate rusty key and a letter with a wax seal. Andy had put them in his pocket to look at when he got a minute alone, but in all the commotion at the funeral, he had forgotten about them.

Now Andy looked at the letter.

I wonder what he wanted to tell me.

Written on the sealed note was his name, in neat spidery handwriting. Until he had received the note from the attorney, Andy hadn't even known that his grandfather knew he existed! Now that he had a moment to think about it, he found his curiosity growing. Why had he been left a key? What did it open? And what in the world could his grandfather have written to him?

Chapter Two
The Letter

I *can't just sit here forever,* Andy thought, staring at the note and the key on the table in front of him. *I should open it.*

Taking a deep, steadying breath, Andy reached for the letter. He examined it closely.

My name's been written with a fountain pen, Andy thought, a smile spreading over his face. Andy had loved fountain pens for as long as he could remember. He had personally collected over thirty of them and was a subscriber to *Fountain Pen Monthly*. Andy loved the way the ink flowed on a crisp, clean sheet of paper. And he loved how elegant everything written with a fountain pen looked.

Sometimes Andy liked to imagine that he was an important man signing an important document. He practiced his signature over and over until he had it just right, every letter the correct size, the flourishes rolling beneath his name with a confident swirl. He could name all the different nibs and what they were used for, list the pros and cons of dropper-filled pens and cartridge fillers, and recite the history of fountain pen usage.

He even knew that the very first fountain pen in recorded history had been commissioned in the tenth century by al-Mu'izz li-Dīn Allah, the caliph of the Maghreb, but he usually didn't mention that to his friends for fear they would think him a little too obsessed.

Andy studied his name. He could tell from the width of the line and the way the ink reacted to the paper the kind of ink and nib his grandfather had used.

Beecham's India Ink and a Hodges HB-2 pen. Wow. That's rare.

Andy had read all about Hodges pens. They were so highly coveted by collectors that even pens in poor condition were often valued at well over ten thousand dollars. Andy's dream was to own one someday. He couldn't care less about getting a new bicycle. He would much rather have a Hodges pen!

Andy broke the crimson wax seal and gently lifted the top of the folded page. His heart beat wildly as he studied the first few lines.

DEAREST ANDY,

My sincerest apologies for not writing sooner or making the time to meet you over the years. As your mother can probably attest, I am an incredibly busy man and I tend to get absorbed in my work.

Although I haven't been able to see you

PERSONALLY, REST ASSURED I have made it my mission to know you. I have had my associates watching over you and reporting back to me for some time. They tell me that you clearly possess the Lostmore Spirit—something that skipped a generation with your mother—and that my trust in you is well placed.

"The Lostmore Spirit? What would make him think I have that?" Andy mumbled.

At this very moment I find myself half-wrapped in fragrant vines, awaiting entry to a temple hidden deep in the Amazonian jungle.

I suspect that my enemies are pursuing me and that the temple I'm investigating may lead to a trap. In spite of the obvious danger, I am, as always, trying my best to keep my head about me.

I'm sure you have probably heard some

strange tales about your old grandfather. After
all, I have seen many unexplainable things—
phenomena that would make your hair stand on
end and your toes curl! (By the way, if you ever
are plagued with such an affliction, a tablespoon
of honey mixed with FARNSWORTH root will relax
your toes and hair and return them to normal.)
And you must be wondering about the key I
left you. It has been designed to open a very
special door—one that hides behind it a mission
of great urgency. I expect the very thought of
danger and adventure will excite you, much as
it did me at your age.

I feel certain that with a little deduction
and logical reasoning, you will be able to quite
easily discover the location of the lock and
thenceforth reveal the amazing quest that
awaits you.

One bit of advice: don't lose your head! It
is a valuable tool and should be treated with

CARE. HEAVEN KNOWS I'VE GOTTEN A TREMENDOUS AMOUNT OF USE FROM MINE AND PLAN TO CONTINUE USING IT FOR MANY YEARS TO COME, IN SPITE OF THE RATHER PERILOUS CIRCUMSTANCES I CURRENTLY FIND MYSELF IN.

Chin up, old boy! Adventure awaits!

Yours sincerely,

Your grandfather

Ned Lostmore

P.S. I look forward to making your acquaintance!

Kungaloosh!

Andy folded the letter up. *Make my acquaintance? We just had his funeral!*

He set the letter back on the table and picked up the rusted key. He shivered. One end of the key was shaped like a human skull.

I'm not really sure I want to know what this opens, he thought. And for the briefest moment, he considered forgetting about the whole thing. He could just return home and keep the key in a drawer somewhere, write the whole thing off as a prank, and go on living a normal, relatively safe existence.

But perhaps there was a little bit more of his grandfather in him than Andy would've liked to admit. The stir of curiosity he felt was hard to resist, and he knew that if he didn't at least try to find the lock, he would always wonder what might have happened.

Maybe I really do have some of that Lostmore Spirit he mentioned, Andy thought.

He stood up and carefully walked toward the blackened stone fireplace. Picture after picture—all showing the same three people—lined the mantel. Andy easily recognized his grandfather, but the other people were a mystery. Who were the man and woman standing beside Ned in all the photos?

Andy looked closer. In almost every photo, the man and woman wore matching safari outfits and pith helmets. She was a stunning beauty with blond hair and a heart-shaped face. He was stocky and seemed as solid and immovable as a boulder.

As Andy took a step back to study the pictures, his knee bumped into a small table with a fragile-looking teacup on it.

Usually when this kind of thing happened (as it did on a daily basis), the outcome would be the table flipping over and the teacup smashing into a million pieces on the floor. Andy would feel his usual embarrassment and frustration with himself for not being more careful and aware of his surroundings. He would immediately start cleaning up the mess, apologizing profusely to the disappointed person whose item he'd broken. And he would, of course, volunteer to pay for the damaged item, usually receiving a forced smile and assurances that all was well. Then Andy would feel miserable for the rest of the day.

But that day, something happened that had never happened before. Andy's right hand shot out with a strange reflexive precision, catching the teacup and its saucer, while his left caught the table a mere inch above the floor.

After carefully setting the table and teacup back in place, Andy stared at his hands in amazement. Phrases like *good catch* and *nice save* were never directed at him, but there was no other way to describe his move.

Andy smiled, feeling a wave of relief and a flash of confidence followed immediately by confusion. What had just happened?

He gazed around the room, noting the dust motes that floated in the late-afternoon sunbeams pouring through the panes of his grandfather's cut-glass windows. Clearly the storm that had been brewing had passed. The warm glow suffusing the study made the room seem almost magical.

Something about Andy felt different. Could it have been that the day's events, although disturbing, had filled him with the conviction that life wasn't meant to be lived so anxiously? Risking everything was something that, until that moment, Andy had read about in his grandfather's books but had never considered doing himself.

It's like the spirit of my grandfather could walk in through the door at any minute and sit down at his desk, he thought.

Andy looked at the array of items lining his grandfather's desk: a letter opener made from a medieval fork, a magnifying glass with a strange horn for a handle, and handwritten list after handwritten list. A 1938 calendar with a series of appointments written all over it in red ink stood in the corner of the desk. Andy smiled, picturing the old jungle doctor hard at work, cataloging his archaeological finds.

Suddenly, Andy noticed a large map displayed above the desk. He walked over to it, narrowly avoiding tripping over an antique brass spittoon that lurked near the bottom corner of the desk.

As Andy drew closer, his eyes widened with surprise. It was not a map of the world, as he'd assumed. In fact, it didn't seem to be a map at all. Instead, it was a huge piece of parchment inscribed with tiny writing designed

to look like continents. As Andy leaned in, he saw that the spidery scrawl was the same as he'd seen on the letter from his grandfather. It had also been written with a fountain pen.

"That looks like a .35-millimeter Humbolt," Andy murmured, observing the tininess of the lettering and thinking of the corresponding pen nib. The writing was precise and beautiful, but try as he might, Andy couldn't read the words. They were all gibberish.

KISREID EIHIT NRO DINRAATAS

The nonsensical phrase was written repeatedly all over the parchment. Andy wondered if it was some kind of Norwegian dialect.

He continued to stare at the words, reciting them over and over. They didn't sound right to him, and he felt like he was missing something. There was a distinctive quality about the phrase that nagged at him, like the answer to a riddle that sat on the tip of his tongue.

Andy loved code breaking. He had read tons of books about it and had even made up his own secret codes. He was sure that what he was looking at was no different from the other codes he had read about. But the solution eluded him. After ten solid minutes of staring at the words, Andy gave up. But no sooner had he turned away from the strange writing than a thought occurred to him.

He wheeled back around, a huge grin spreading over his face. The elegant simplicity of what his grandfather had done filled him with newfound respect for the man.

So simple, Andy thought. *It's almost a joke!*

But it wasn't a joke. It was an instruction!

If he skipped every other letter of each word and reversed the order of the remaining letters, the command revealed itself. *Kisreid eihit nro dinraatas* became *stand on the desk.*

Andy turned from the map and cleared off the top of his grandfather's desk. He pulled himself up and surveyed the room from a new height, his jaw dropping in wonder. The room, which had seemed so cluttered and disorganized from the ground, had changed. From this new angle, all the furniture and artifacts formed a carefully organized pattern.

"Amazing," Andy whispered, awestruck.

Subtle golden lines had been painted on the surfaces of the artifacts and furniture. The light pouring through the windows illuminated the lines.

Andy was breathless with excitement. He observed the lines closely.

There's a whole other world here, he thought.

Then he noticed something else. All the lines pointed to the same object: a tiny painting of a gold key on top of a display cabinet filled with pinned moths. The head of the key was pointing directly at . . .

"That suit of samurai armor!" Andy exclaimed.

The armor stood in the corner of the room, next to a large brass vase holding a spiky cluster of decorative tribal spears.

That must be where the keyhole is hidden, Andy thought.

He hopped off the desk, sending a boxful of paper clips scattering to the floor. Then, being extra careful not to bump anything else, he moved across the room to the armor. His pulse quickened. He had to admit his grandfather might have been right. This *was* pretty exciting. Maybe he was up for an adventure after all.

At least, as long as having an adventure is more like finding an Easter egg hidden in a house than having a near-death experience in the jungle, he reminded himself.

As he examined the suit of armor, Andy noticed a sequence of silver numbers engraved on its black marble base.

21 14 4 5 18   13 5

I wonder if there's some kind of combination lock somewhere, Andy thought. He searched around the base but found nothing interesting other than a tiny etched skull at the end of the numerical sequence.

Andy studied the key again. "The symbol matches the key," he told himself, "so I must be on the right track." Andy ran his hand through his thatch of blond hair and whistled through his teeth. If this was a code of some kind, it was tougher than the last one.

He'd never been a math wiz, but he could tell that the numbers weren't arranged in any kind of mathematical order based on prime numbers.

"Hmmm, I wonder why Grandfather used numbers instead of words this time," Andy mused. He stared at the numbers for another long moment. There was a small gap between the first five numbers and the last two.

"It's almost like words. . . ."

He snapped his fingers as a new thought popped into his head.

"Of course!" he exclaimed. Andy mentally counted through the alphabet, assigning each number its corresponding letter. After finishing, he realized that the numbers did indeed spell out two simple words.

UNDER ME.

Under what . . . the suit of armor? Or does it mean something else? he wondered.

Andy tried feeling all around the base of the armor, searching for any visible cracks or a way to get underneath it. But after a few seconds, he concluded that it was solidly fixed to the floor.

Hmmm.

Again he noticed the skull next to the numbers. Could the phrase be about that? Maybe he was supposed to find something beneath it.

Andy placed the edge of his fingernail under the tiny raised skull and pulled upward. To his delight, it opened with a little pop and revealed a keyhole.

Yes!

Andy grinned as he pulled the key out of his pocket and placed it in the lock.

Here goes nothing.

Chapter Three
The Mysterious Staircase

The key turned with a smooth click. Andy waited, but nothing happened. *What went wrong?* he wondered.

Then, to Andy's surprise, the suit of armor swiveled with a grinding noise, revealing a roughly cut hole beneath its base.

Whoa! Andy gazed at a series of stone steps that descended into total darkness.

A gust of musty air blew upward, lightly riffling his hair. The passage smelled of damp earth and mold.

Andy hesitated. *Should I really do this? Anything could be down there! What if it's dangerous?*

Andy glanced back at the doorway that led from his grandfather's study to the rest of the house. It wasn't too late to forget the whole thing and go find his parents. But the tiniest flicker of newfound courage burned inside him. He couldn't help wondering what was down there. What was the mission he was supposed to undertake?

With a deep, steadying breath, Andy stepped into the dark passage. Keeping his hand against the wall, he tentatively walked down the first few stairs, assuring himself that if he ran into anything scary, he could always turn around. He hadn't gone much farther when the suit of armor began rumbling back into place.

Andy shrieked and tried to dash back up and out the opening. Before he'd taken three steps, he slipped and banged his shin painfully on the stone stairs.

Andy hardly noticed the discomfort.

"No!" he shouted as the base of the statue groaned back into place with a resounding boom. The last crack of light from the library disappeared above him. The heavy silence and oppressive darkness that followed weighed down on him like a suffocating blanket. He had never been more frightened in his life!

His breath came in short, ragged gasps. He felt like he was hyperventilating.

No one knows I'm down here! Why didn't I tell someone what I was doing?

Andy tried to catch his breath, but it seemed impossible. Feeling his way through the darkness, he slowly started to crawl toward the top of the stairs. His mind filled with horrible images of being trapped in the dark forever.

Please don't be locked. Please...

His fingers probed the bottom of the statue's base, groping for a keyhole. But his worst fears were confirmed. All he could feel was the rough-hewn base, with no apparent way to unlock it from underneath.

Andy shoved until his arms shook, but the statue didn't budge. His heart sank as he leaned against the wall by the stairs.

"Help!" he called. "Somebody, please help me!"

But his voice was muffled by the closeness of the chamber, and judging by the lack of light coming into the stairwell, he guessed there wasn't much sound getting out. Andy tried again to calm his shaking nerves. "If I can't go back up, then the only other choice is to go down," he muttered. He rose and—rubbing his sore leg—started to turn around.

No sooner had he decided to push on than a warm light filled the stairwell.

Andy glanced at the walls of the stone stairway, relieved to see small torches spaced at regular intervals. He didn't know how they'd been lit, but they made him feel much better about his situation.

At least I can see where I'm going, he thought.

Andy slid his hand along the rough stone wall for support as he shakily descended the narrow staircase.

"How far does this thing go down?" he mumbled.

After several minutes, he reached the bottom. To his surprise, the air wasn't stuffy or dank, like he would have expected so far underground. Instead, it was dry and rather warm.

Andy stared down a long hallway that stretched in front of him. Side passages led off to the right and left, and he noticed highly polished wooden rails with brass fittings attached to the walls.

His palms were sweaty, and he wiped them repeatedly on the front of his trousers, then took careful hold of the railing and continued forward. A mysterious light glowed from somewhere around the corner.

I hope I'm going the right way. What if I get lost down here?

Andy was interrupted by a strange smell. It was a scent so powerful and exotic that it momentarily banished all other thoughts from his mind.

Pineapple? Who in the world would be eating pineapple so deep underground?

The fruity aroma made Andy's stomach contract with hunger, and he pushed forward, eager to find the source of the delicious smell. How long had it been since he'd eaten anything?

Andy turned the corner and stopped short. He had stepped into a giant open cavern. The space had been converted into the most incredible, most *massive* library he had ever seen. Leather-bound books lined the walls. To one side stood a roaring fireplace, complete with cozy chairs surrounding the blazing hearth.

Andy felt a sense of calm wash over him. There was nothing he loved more than curling up with a good book. What could go wrong in a beautiful library? Then he noticed the other *thing* in the room. It towered over him, practically seven feet tall. Its body was crafted from some kind of blackened metal, and its face held two glowing lightbulbs for eyes, a long pointed metal nose, and a round hole covered with wire mesh for a mouth.

Strangest of all, the creature held a tray containing fresh slices of pineapple upside-down cake.

Andy's stomach grumbled again, and he forced himself to take another step forward. *Can it see me?* he wondered as he stared up into the lightbulb eyes.

As he drew closer, Andy heard the whirring of clock-work machinery coming from somewhere deep inside the creature. *It's a robot!* he thought. But though it continued to whir, the automaton didn't move.

Andy considered whether he should take a slice of cake.

It looks like it's offering it to me, he thought. *But what if it's some kind of test? Maybe I'm not supposed to touch it.*

He stood there for a moment, wrestling with what he should do. The tests his grandfather had put in place were like puzzles.

Nothing in this place exists without a reason, he thought. *I must be meant to eat it.*

Andy cautiously took a slice of cake from the tray

and—without removing his eyes from the robot—took a bite.

The warm, sweet cake was every bit as good as it smelled!

Andy was still savoring it when the robot, which had been standing as still as a statue, suddenly turned and walked away. A moment later it reappeared and offered him a cup of tea.

Andy sipped the aromatic brew as he observed the strange robot. He had read his fair share of science fiction and adventure magazines, but he'd never expected to encounter anything like this. Who had built it? Did it belong to his grandfather? And more important, why was it standing in the middle of a vast library?

Andy finished his tea and asked, "Can you understand me?"

There was an almost inaudible click and the robot nodded once. Andy grinned.

"Did you belong to my grandfather?"

There was a second click, followed by another nod.

Andy felt his heartbeat quicken. How had Ned come by such an amazing machine? Andy was starting to realize there was a lot more to his grandfather than even his books let on. It seemed like just when he thought he'd found out the most extraordinary thing about his grandfather, there was something more to uncover.

A thought occurred to Andy as he gazed into the metal face. "Do you know who I am?" he asked.

There was another click. This time, instead of nodding, the metallic man emitted a sound like radio static. From somewhere deep inside the robot, a voice replied, "You are Andy Stanley, grandson of Ned Lostmore. My name is Boltonhouse. I am pleased to make your acquaintance."

"Likewise," Andy replied. "Er, my grandfather left instructions for me to come down here. Do you know what I'm supposed to do?"

Boltonhouse didn't respond. The metal man just stood there, as if waiting for a different command.

"Ned Lostmore gave me a key," Andy said, trying again. "What is my next task?"

Still nothing.

Andy thought for a moment and realized that everything he'd figured out so far had come through his ability to decipher clues. He turned his attention to the massive library. The next clue must be there somewhere.

Andy sighed as he took in the size of the library. It seemed that his grandfather wasn't fond of easy answers.

Andy walked past Boltonhouse and made his way to the nearest aisle. He loved libraries. While other children craved new bicycles, bags of marbles, and slingshots, all Andy ever wanted was another book. He loved to run his fingers down a cover, tracing the outline of the title. He would crack it open and breathe in the dry, dusty smell of its interior.

Andy had always preferred books to people. He was a quiet boy, and he usually found himself at a loss for words when it came to making conversation with his peers at school. But in a book, he could get lost. He could forget the boys who laughed at him for his clumsiness and for his inability in sports.

As Andy made his way down the aisles, his gaze fell on the unusual titles written on the spines of the leather-bound tomes. He brushed the edges of the books with his fingers, noting each one as he passed. He didn't know exactly what he was looking for, but he hoped that if he remained open-minded, the right book would jump out at him. Andy had been down three of the mazelike aisles when he passed a row of books that looked especially worn and tattered.

Everest Exhibition: In Search of the Yeti. The Skipper Handbook for River Navigation. Profiles of Legendary Pirates of the Caribbean. Parrots as Pets. The Friendship Pineapple. Fix Anything with a Monkey Wrench...

All of them sounded interesting. Had he been anywhere else, he would have grabbed the nearest one, plopped down by the fire, and lost himself in his favorite blissful pastime. But now was not the time for that. Somewhere down there was a clue, and if he ever wanted to get out of that subterranean maze, he had to find it!

Andy reached into his pocket and felt the weight of the key his grandfather had left him. He drew it out and studied it again. The key had gotten him down there, but what he was supposed to do now that he had arrived?

As Andy tucked the key back into his pocket, he gazed around the library. It would take days to read every title of every book there. And he didn't even know what he was looking for.

Suddenly, Andy's eye fell on a small golden statue positioned on a table at the end of a row of bookcases. *What is that? And what's it doing down here?*

Andy walked over and took a closer look. The statue seemed out of place in the library. It was of a queen sitting on a throne. The woman looked exotic, with long hair and a flower lei around her neck. The word FIBONACCI was inscribed on the base of her throne.

Andy looked at the statue, perplexed. *Leis are*

usually Hawaiian. But the name Fibonacci doesn't sound Hawaiian. I wonder who this is supposed to be.

Andy picked up the statue and turned it over and over. In one hand, the queen held a loaf of bread that sparkled with what looked like tiny diamonds. In her other hand she held what looked like a pepper.

Andy tilted the statue and noticed something odd carved into the bottom of it. He traced his finger over a grouping of pockmarks and scratches.

Andy was sure it was a clue. He just wasn't quite seeing what he was supposed to.

I know I've seen something like this before, but where was it? Andy thought. *The scratches seem familiar, like they're a pattern of some kind.*

Suddenly, he realized what he was looking at. Andy shook his head. Why hadn't he figured it out earlier? Morse code was one of the most famous codes in existence. His code breaker magazines used it all the time. Andy had even written notes in it himself. He quickly translated the message.

" '*Ananas comosus.*' Now what in the world does *that* mean?"

Andy was about to look for a dictionary—a task he knew could take ages to complete there—when he had an idea. He called back down the aisle, "Boltonhouse, can you help me find a book?"

The robot immediately turned and walked over to him. *So that's what he's for,* Andy thought. *He's a librarian!*

Andy looked up at the robot. "Does this library have a reference section?" he asked.

The mechanical servant nodded once and set off. Andy hurried close behind. After several moments, Boltonhouse stopped in front of a shelf filled with dictionaries and encyclopedias.

Andy was about to thank Boltonhouse when he saw that the mechanical man had already walked away.

"Okay, let's see here," Andy said as he pulled down a dictionary. "*Ananas comosus.* It sounds Latin."

Andy searched the book. "*Ananas . . . Ananas . . .* It's not here." Andy sighed, but he wasn't ready to give up. "Okay, how about *comosus*?" He flipped through the pages. "Here it is! Hmmm . . . tufted or crowned."

At least Andy had defined half of the phrase. He rolled the other half around in his mind. What could it mean? "*Ananas . . . Ananas . . .* Kind of sounds like bananas." He stared at the ceiling, lost in thought. "Tufted bananas? Tufted fruit?"

Suddenly, a thought struck him. He turned to an encyclopedia and pulled out the volume labeled *P-R*. He blew away a coating of dust, then flipped through it until he reached the page he was looking for.

"'One of the outstanding traits of the pineapple, or *Ananas comosus*, is that its unique exterior pattern can be divided into the Fibonacci sequence of numbers: 1, 1, 2, 3, 5, 8, 13, 21,'" he read aloud.

Andy's breathing quickened. The book went on to explain that the Fibonacci sequence was a series of numbers that happened repeatedly in nature, dividing the bodies of various plant and animal forms into unique patterns.

"That's why the word *Fibonacci* is on the base of the statue," he whispered. He read on: "'Varieties of the pineapple include the smooth cayenne, sugarloaf, and queen.'"

Andy thought about the statue and the items that were represented there.

"The pepper and the loaf held by a queen," Andy said. "That's it! The clue must have something to do with a pineapple!"

He thought about the warm pineapple upside-down cake Boltonhouse had greeted him with when he'd entered the library. It all made sense!

"Okay, Grandfather . . . what did you mean by leaving the word *pineapple* as a clue?" he wondered aloud.

Andy flipped through the pages of the encyclopedia. The most obvious place to hide the next clue would have been inside the book, but he didn't see anything unusual.

Andy paced, trying to figure out what to do next.

"Pineapple . . . pineapple . . . why a pineapple?" he muttered. He walked down an aisle, patting his forehead repeatedly. "Come on, Andy. Think!"

As Andy turned into the aisle with the statue at the end of it, he remembered something he'd seen before. He looked over the titles of the books again. *"Everest Expedition: In Search of the Yeti. Parrots as Pets. The Friendship Pineapple."*

Andy smiled slyly as he pulled the book from the shelf. He trailed his fingers along the battered lemon-colored leather and stared at the small image of a pineapple embossed in the center. The cover was unremarkable, almost overlookable. Holding his breath, Andy opened the book.

Something large and metal clattered to the floor with a loud, rattling *clank!*

Andy bent down to pick it up. It was another key! This one was very different from the first he'd inherited. It had a pineapple carved into a brass handle, which gleamed brightly.

Bingo.

Andy turned the key over. The shaft had a tiny inscription written on it. "'Use the key,'" Andy read. He snorted. "Well, that seems pretty obvious."

He decided to check out the contents of the book and was surprised to see that it had nothing to do with pineapples at all. Instead, it contained a map of the library along with a series of entries—all of which, Andy noticed, had been inscribed with the same fountain pen nib that had been used to create the clever map in his grandfather's study.

"You can't stump me, Grandfather," he whispered with a smile. "I'm on to your tricks."

Andy noticed that the top of the map was inscribed with the name and logo of the Jungle Explorers' Society. The famous society was an elite group of men and women who were interested in the discovery and preservation of the world's most precious treasures and artifacts. The Society published a journal that was known for its stunning photographs of far-off lands and

THE
JUNGLE EXPLORER'S
SOCIETY

Key

Entrance

insightful articles about indigenous peoples. A copy of the Society's journal could be bought for a quarter at almost any newsstand in the world—which Andy delighted in as he eagerly handed over his money every month.

Little else was known about the group, and Andy had always suspected there was more to them than met the eye. He'd read a lot about secret societies and knew that such groups as the Freemasons, the Illuminati, the Rosicrucian Order, and the Thaumaturgic Cartographers all had both public and private personas.

Andy had been collecting the Society's journals for as long as he could remember and had always secretly wished that he could be a member.

Andy moved his fingers across the page, studying it closely. It was a fairly ordinary map, well drawn and accurate. All the bookshelves and the fireplace in the library were perfectly depicted. There was even a tiny drawing of Boltonhouse standing where Andy had first seen him when he entered the room. Next to the drawing of the robot, so small that Andy had to squint to see it, was a pineapple symbol.

"Eureka!" Andy exclaimed.

Boltonhouse called out to him. "Master Andy."

Andy turned. "Yes, Boltonhouse?"

"Your grandfather is waiting for you," Boltonhouse replied calmly.

Andy stared at the automaton, confused. "My grandfather is dead," he said.

"Your grandfather is waiting for you," the robot repeated.

Andy felt a chill go up his spine. What was the machine talking about? He had obviously been programmed a long time ago, when Andy's grandfather was still alive. Did he really believe that Ned Lostmore was somewhere in the mansion?

"You're in communication with my grandfather?" Andy asked.

"Affirmative," Boltonhouse replied.

"Then why can't I hear him?" Andy asked.

As soon as he'd asked the question, a thought popped into his mind. Was it possible that Boltonhouse was some kind of medium and was communicating with his grandfather's *ghost*?

As if he knew what Andy was thinking, Boltonhouse added, "Your grandfather is very much alive, although he is much *changed*. He is waiting for you."

The automaton took several steps forward and reached out his hand. On it was an iron key ring. "You must collect all of your grandfather's keys. You are the new Keymaster. Your grandfather is waiting."

Keymaster? What does that mean? Andy wondered.

Seeing no choice, Andy took the offered key ring and added the two keys his grandfather had left for him. The ring had a small clasp that allowed Andy to clip it to his belt.

I have no idea what all of this means, he thought. *But I have to find out! Why did Boltonhouse call me the Keymaster? And could Grandfather really be alive?*

Andy was terrified of what might be waiting for him,

and he was growing more nervous by the second, but in spite of that, he was also growing incredibly curious. He knew if he didn't go through with the mission, he'd always wonder what would have happened. Besides, he couldn't go back the way he'd come. There was no exit in that direction.

Andy didn't know what Boltonhouse meant when he said that Andy's grandfather was changed, but he suspected it didn't mean he was a ghost. That left only one option: Ned Lostmore was alive. And it seemed he needed Andy's help.

"If I really do have the Lostmore Spirit, then now's a good time to test it," he murmured.

Andy remembered where he'd seen the pineapple symbol on the map of the library. Tucking the book under his arm, he walked down the aisles, threading his way through the massive maze of shelves until he reached a small alcove near the corner of the room.

At first he was surprised to see nothing but a plain-looking wall. Then, a few inches off the floor, he spotted a small brass keyhole with a pineapple symbol above it.

Andy retrieved the pineapple key from his belt and inserted it into the lock. He exhaled slowly. This was it: time to meet the grandfather he'd only read about— or not.

To his surprise, nothing happened. The key wouldn't budge.

"Come on," Andy coaxed. But try as he might to turn it, the key still would not move.

Andy took the key out of the keyhole and examined it closely. "Doesn't seem to be bent," he mumbled, turning it over. Then he noticed again the writing on the shaft of the key.

Use the key.

"I'm trying to!" he shouted. He was about to insert the key into the lock and try again when he had an idea.

So far, none of the clues his grandfather had left him had been easy to figure out. Just going to the place indicated on the map was too obvious. What if . . .

Andy opened the book and examined the map

inside. His eyes darted to the bottom of the page, where a small group of symbols was located. Next to the series of symbols was the word *Key*.

"Tricky," Andy said, grinning. He knew that the word *key* meant more than one thing, but its second meaning hadn't occurred to him until then. If he was right about his hunch, then the inscription on the key referred to the key used to interpret the symbols written on the map.

Maybe this keyhole is a fake, meant to keep intruders from finding the real one, Andy thought. *Someone else might try the lock, find out that the key didn't work, and give up. But not me!*

Andy noticed that one of the symbols printed on the map key was the same as the tiny pineapple he'd followed to the keyhole. Next to it was an X.

Andy eagerly searched the map for anything resembling an X. That must be the location of the real keyhole! But the map showed no such symbol.

Taking the book with him, he moved around the library, searching down every aisle. He mentally checked off each one, not finding what he was looking for. When he got to the opposite side of the library, he stopped short. Against the wall was a large African shield with two crossed spears behind it.

X marks the spot!

Andy felt carefully along the shield's edge. At first it seemed like nothing was there. But when he tilted the shield a little bit to the left . . .

There it is! The keyhole!

With his hands shaking, he inserted the pineapple key in the lock.

Here we go. . . .

This time, the key turned smoothly.

Chapter Four
Into the Secret Chamber

The door was so cleverly hidden that Andy never would have suspected it was there. But after he turned the key, the thin outline of an entryway appeared next to the shield, and a section of the wall swung open.

A sloping floor stretched into complete blackness in front of Andy, and a damp, unpleasant smell emanated from the passage. He tried to push images of tombs and haunted houses out of his mind. Seeing several spider-webs near the inside of the opening didn't help, and he couldn't keep from thinking, *If there really are such things as ghosts, this seems like the perfect place for them to haunt.*

Andy suppressed a shudder. Then, telling himself it was best not to think about it, he pushed forward into the darkness.

"There's no such thing as ghosts. . . . There's no such thing as ghosts . . ." Andy mumbled as he walked. "It's only a dark hallway, nothing more." Intention-ally walking into the darkness was better than being unexpectedly plunged into it, as he had been on the stairs to the library, but the darkness itself was no less disconcerting.

As he groped his way along the stone wall, wishing he had brought a flashlight or a lantern with him, the tiny amount of courage his curiosity had supplied him with quickly faded. He couldn't see a thing, and the thought of the horrors he might be passing gave him the shivers.

He had been walking for some time when someone with a strong voice and an English accent called out, "Is that you, Andy?"

Andy stopped, paralyzed with fear.

"Who's there?" he whispered. "And how do you know my name?"

He heard a loud chuckle. As far as he was concerned, there was nothing humorous about the situation he found himself in. Why did the mysterious voice sound so merry?

"If that's Andy, this is his grandfather," the voice answered. "I've been waiting for you."

He certainly doesn't sound *dead*, Andy thought.

Andy was about to answer the mysterious voice when, suddenly, a bright light filled the room. He threw up his arm to shield his eyes. Then, feeling foolish, he slowly lowered it. The light was not so bright after all. In fact, it was rather soft. It was only the suddenness of it that had surprised Andy. Now, looking around, he saw that it was coming from a glass-enclosed cabinet.

Andy drew closer, then stopped short. The cabinet held what seemed to be a collection of items left over from a jungle expedition: a worn pith helmet, an open book, a pair of binoculars, a British flag. But none of those objects captured Andy's attention. It was the thing hanging in the center of the cabinet that froze him in his tracks.

Andy's jaw dropped, and he felt suspended somewhere between horror and astonishment.

"It can't be. . . ."

The object was a shrunken head!

Even worse, the head was familiar. Andy had spent years looking at photos of its mischievous face on the backs of books. So as much as he might like to deny it, he could not hide from the fact that the shrunken head staring back at him was none other than Ned Lostmore's.

"Grandfather, is that you?" Andy asked in a shaky voice.

He gawked at the small head, with its thatch of wild white hair sticking straight up. Ned's long side-burns extended almost to his chin, and a curling white mustache sat above his lip. A pair of twinkling blue eyes gazed back at Andy, the left one covered by a monocle.

And then the shrunken head spoke.

"Andy, my boy! I knew you'd find me! Well done!"

Andy nearly fainted from shock. How could Ned—reduced to no more than a head on a string—still be alive and *talking* to him?

"Grandfather? Your head . . . How . . . ?" Andy started when he regained his senses.

"Ah, yes," Ned said with another chuckle. "The unfortunate result of an encounter with a witch doctor by the name of Bungalow Bob. It appears my enemies wanted to get their hands on some powerful ancient artifacts I was protecting. My own fault, really. I was so focused on gaining entry to that temple I never saw Bob coming."

"He shrank your head?" Andy asked. "But . . . but

doesn't that mean that first you were . . . you know . . ."

He couldn't bring himself to say the word *dead*, but Ned got the gist of his grandson's concern.

"There are many types of magic in the jungle, some more mysterious than science can readily supply us answers to," Ned explained lightly. "Suffice to say, I am still very much alive. I have merely been *transformed*. I am not a small-minded man about such things as the mystical, my dear boy. Surely you must have been able to deduce that from my writings."

Ned burst into another fit of delighted chuckles. "Small-minded! Ha! That describes me to a tee."

The quip sent his head bobbing.

Andy, too stunned to find *anything* funny, stared at his grandfather's head bobbing on its string. *Okay, just stay calm*, he told himself. *Yes, this is strange, and, yes, Grandfather is a talking shrunken head. But he's still Ned Lostmore. You're finally getting to meet your grandfather. Isn't that what you always wanted?*

Andy still couldn't quite believe what was happening,

but his anxiety was gradually giving way to excitement. He had so many questions that he hardly knew where to begin.

"Why—" Andy began.

"*Why?*" Ned interrupted. "Yes indeed, 'Why?' is one of the most important questions there is. *Why* are you here? *Why* did my enemies do this to me? *Why* is there no cure for the Jamaican fungal worm's digestive issues? *Why* does the nose hair of the Amazonian leaf monkey cure itchy feet? Why? Why? Why?

"*Why* is one reason I brought you here. Of course, there are other questions, too, such as 'What?,' 'How?,' and 'Where?' But let's focus on 'Why?'" Ned fixed Andy with a meaningful stare. "Why did I bring you here? The reason, my dear boy, is that although you may not have realized it, I have been watching over you for a long time. I have a wide variety of colleagues, and they have supplied me over the years with regular reports of your progress," Ned continued. "Needless to say, I see in you much of myself when I was your age. I suspect you crave adventure nearly as much as I did. And, as luck would have it, I have a mission for you that will be quite dangerous."

Andy looked at his grandfather skeptically. "But . . . you're wrong. I'm nothing like you. I'm not an adventurer! I . . . I just read about them in books."

"Books?" said Ned. "Books are meant for writing your own courageous deeds, not reading about someone else's. Wouldn't you rather live the adventure than read about it?"

"I'm clumsy, Grandfather," Andy blurted out. "And I . . . I've never been very athletic. I don't know a single thing about jungle medicine or how to make your head . . . um . . . un-shrunk. I just don't think I'm . . . well . . . qualified."

"First of all, dear boy," Ned said, "when someone asks you if you'd like to go on an adventure, the correct answer is always 'Absolutely!' And secondly, I'm quite happy with my current state. I have plenty of time for writing, and I enjoy *hanging around*," he said. "Ha!

There's nothing more dangerous than developing a big head. Ask anyone! No, it is not restoring myself to my former glory that I'm talking about. I need your assistance in retrieving something of grave importance to the safety of the entire world."

Ned offered his grandson a wink, one that was magnified hugely by his monocle. "And as far as your being qualified? Well, sometimes one has to be given a chance to prove what he's truly capable of."

Chapter Five
The Quest

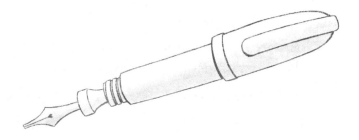

Andy was about to argue his lack of qualifications again when Boltonhouse appeared, holding something that made all other thoughts fly out of Andy's mind. It was the most beautiful fountain pen Andy had ever seen. Taking the pen, he examined it closely.

"A Hodges A-7400 Zoomwriter special edition!" Andy exclaimed breathlessly, turning it over delicately in his hand. "There were only ten of these ever made!"

Andy looked up at his grandfather. "And it's got an eighteen-karat-gold .35-millimeter Humbolt nib. This pen must be worth a fortune!"

"You really do know your writing instruments!" Ned said. "But there's far more to that pen than meets the eye, dear boy. Its value cannot be overestimated when it comes to self-defense."

"What do you mean?" Andy asked. He stared at the gorgeous pen, admiring its jade-green barrel and ebony cap. It looked innocuous enough—for a priceless fountain pen.

"I'll be sending you to the tropics—a land of powerful myths and even more powerful magic," Ned explained. "The normal rules you've led yourself to believe about the world you live in don't apply there. In fact, they're downright ridiculous! That means you'll be needing protection, and only the finest in self-defense weaponry will do."

Ned grinned, displaying a row of tiny, perfectly white teeth. "Now, if you remove the cap and place it on the back of the pen, you'll see one of the finest writing instruments ever made. But if you were to twist the cap to the right and press down on the back of the pen . . ."

Andy did as his grandfather suggested. There was a loud bang, and Andy fell backward with a shout, nearly tripping over Boltonhouse. As he shakily regained his balance, he noticed a nearby antique cabinet had been knocked over by the blast.

"Wh-what was that?" Andy asked.

"An atomic pulse emitter," Ned replied matter-of-factly. "It's affectionately known as a monkey gun by my colleagues in the scientific community. This is because its abbreviation spells *ape*. But trust me, my boy: it won't make a monkey out of anyone who uses it. Ha!"

Andy stared down at the pen. *I'd better be careful with this thing! What if I forget I turned the cap to the right and accidentally hit the back?*

Andy's hand shook as he twisted the cap to its original position. He was about to give the pen back to Boltonhouse when his grandfather stopped him.

"Half a moment! I haven't shown you what else it can do! Now then, this other function is far more pleasant. Boltonhouse, if you'd be so kind as to supply my grandson with some paper . . ."

Boltonhouse reached into a hidden compartment in his chest and removed a small leather-bound journal. Andy took it cautiously. After his experience with the pen, he wasn't sure he trusted *anything* Boltonhouse gave him.

"In 'writing mode' the pen acts as a very sophisticated wireless telegraph. When you're about to write, simply twist the cap to the left. Every word you produce will then be transmitted back here to me. Go on, give it a try!"

Andy did as his grandfather instructed. As he wrote, he marveled at how wonderfully the ink flowed from the Zoomwriter. *I can't believe I'm writing with one of these. It's so smooth—even better than I imagined!*

As Andy finished writing his name, a clicking sound

came from somewhere inside Boltonhouse's head. Andy recognized the *tap, tap, tapping* of a telegraph being generated. Seconds later, a small piece of paper scrolled out of a slot behind where the robot's ear would have been. The machine tore the small scrap from his head and handed it to Andy. There, printed in neat block letters, was his name: ANDY STANLEY.

"Incredible!" Andy said.

"Indeed it is," Ned replied. "But it's not all the pen can do. The last feature is something *truly* astounding and perhaps the most important to remember. If ever you find yourself in an inescapable situation, press down three times on the cap with all your strength. Help will come."

Andy took a long last look at the pen. Then he closed the cap and reached out to give it back to Boltonhouse, but he was stopped short by his grandfather.

"That's yours, my boy," Ned said.

"What?" Andy asked, confused.

"You heard me. It's yours! You'll need it on your

adventure. What kind of grandfather would I be if I sent you off into a tropical jungle without protection? Consider it a birthday present . . . one that's long overdue."

Andy looked at the Zoomwriter again. He had been so focused on the pen that he'd nearly forgotten about his quest. Anxiety filled him as he thought about what kind of mission could require a telegraph and an exploding pen.

Ned paused to allow Andy another moment to study the pen, then continued: "Whatever you do, don't lose it! I expect you will need it to survive out there."

Andy swallowed nervously. "Survive?" he asked. What exactly did his grandfather have in store for him?

Ned bobbed excitedly. "Oh, to be your age again!" he said. "Why, if I were in your shoes, my boy, I'd be beside myself with excitement!"

Excitement? A new book is exciting. This pen is exciting. The idea of surviving in the jungle is terrifying! What if I get killed? What will I tell my parents?

Andy thought about all the dangerous things in the tropics he'd read about, including gigantic insects and dangerous volcanoes. He felt dizzy and wondered if he was going to faint. His grandfather, taking Andy's unfocused, dazed expression to mean he was overwhelmed with excitement, continued. "Now then, about your first mission . . . I've appointed you as my new Keymaster, and with that—"

"Keymaster?" Andy interrupted, remembering Boltonhouse's earlier words. "What does that mean exactly?"

"The secret society of which I'm a part has a special position reserved for an individual like yourself—someone our enemies would never expect to keep the treasures and artifacts that we protect safe. I have been the Keymaster for well over thirty years, but it has become apparent of late that my role is no longer a secret. I had hoped one day to pass the position on to your mother, but I fear she has none of the Lostmore Spirit. You, on the other hand . . . Our enemies will never suspect a twelve-year-old boy to hold the position of Keymaster."

Ned gave Andy a crooked grin. "You didn't realize that you were being tested when I brought you here. Your finding your way to this room confirmed what I suspected about you: that you are a boy with a keen intellect! Not just anyone could have put the clues together like you did."

Andy felt a flush of pride at his grandfather's words.

"It wasn't easy. You hid the clues really well!" Andy confessed.

"Of course I did! And you performed brilliantly."

His grandfather's praise made Andy wonder if perhaps he did possess the Lostmore Spirit after all. He was still nervous about the quest, but he was beginning to feel a hint of excitement at the idea of taking on the challenge.

"So, as the new Keymaster, what am I supposed to do?" he asked.

"You must keep the keys that protect our treasures safe," Ned explained. "We feared that if the keys were all kept by one individual on a key ring, it would be too great a risk. What if that person were kidnapped and the ring stolen? It would be a disaster! Our enemies would be able to find and use the artifacts for their own diabolical purposes!"

Ned became animated, bouncing on his string with agitation. "That must never happen! Keeping those keys safe often means keeping them hidden. That is why we appoint a Keymaster—to know where every key is and hide them if necessary. It's a position of honor, but also one of great danger. You must never give up the location of the keys, no matter what happens to you. Even if you are captured or tortured by our enemies, you must keep your secrets."

"C-captured and tortured?" Andy stammered. He gulped. He was good at keeping secrets, but being Keymaster sounded dangerous. Would he be able to hold his tongue in the face of torture?

Ned softened a little when he saw how anxious his grandson looked.

"Not to worry, my boy. The Society has been watching you for years and will continue to do so. Your job is to protect the keys. It's our job to protect you."

Andy nodded, trying to push the idea of torture from his mind. He nervously fingered the key ring at his belt.

"Ah, yes, the keys," Ned said. "You must be wondering about them. . . . The one with the skull on the handle is a skeleton key. Very useful. It can be used to open many doors."

Andy nodded. "What about the pineapple key?"

"Ah, that one only unlocks the door that leads to this chamber. You'll want to keep that one handy. I expect you to visit often and to tell me where you intend to hide any keys you may find on your quests."

Andy nodded. "Being Keymaster sounds like a big responsibility."

"One of the biggest," Ned confirmed. "So, will you do this for us?"

For the first time since he'd arrived, Andy was actually being given a choice in the matter.

I could still back out of all this, he thought. *I could just go home and forget about the whole thing.*

But as soon as the thought popped into his mind, he dismissed it. The quest made him nervous, but a thirst for adventure had awoken inside him, and he knew deep down that it was the opportunity of a lifetime.

No more living inside books, he reminded himself. *You've always wondered about your grandfather. Now you finally have a chance to be just like him!*

Andy took a deep breath and stood a little straighter. He stared back at his grandfather with a determined expression. "I give you my word. I'll do my very best not to let you down, Grandfather."

Ned smiled warmly. "Well done. I'm counting on it."

Then Ned's expression grew serious. "Now then, for your first job, I need you to recover a very special key."

Chapter Six
The Airship

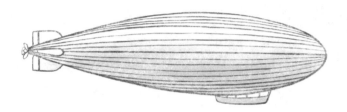

Andy, who was feeling more than ever like he was moving about in a dream, allowed Boltonhouse to escort him to a secret hangar behind his grandfather's mansion. It was a relief to be aboveground again, but he barely had a moment to register the fresh air before he spied a massive silver blimp.

Andy marveled at the pristine ship hovering in the air. Hundreds of ropes tethered the zeppelin to the ground, preventing it from floating away. Andy couldn't stop himself from grinning. He had never flown before, and now he was about to board an airship.

Looks like I'll be taking my first flight in style!

Boltonhouse ushered him toward a large rolling staircase. The next thing Andy knew, he was climbing the stairs to the cockpit.

I can't believe this is actually happening! I'm about to go on a secret mission, and I haven't even packed a toothbrush!

Andy strode to the top of the rolling stairway. The pilot nodded to him in greeting as he entered the cabin, and Andy lifted his hand in a small wave. Suddenly, a thought occurred to him, and he wheeled around and blurted to Boltonhouse, "Wait! I can't go. What would my parents say? I need to tell them where I am!"

Andy heard a clicking sound and then the robot replied, "Not to worry, Andy Stanley. Your mother has been informed that you've decided to stay with your grandfather. She has been told to expect you home in a week."

"My mother knows my grandfather is alive?" Andy asked. "Why didn't she tell me?"

If Boltonhouse knew the answer to the question, he didn't reply.

Andy sighed and gazed around the cabin.

The airship was a marvel of modern construction. Its massive, sleek silver body was designed to cut through the sky as silently as a cloud. The gondola at the bottom of the ship was outfitted with luxurious accommodations. Velvet couches were artfully positioned around the cabin, as were soft leather chairs. There were bookshelves holding publications of every adventure magazine in existence. As Andy took a seat, he was greeted by a private chef who offered to prepare anything he could imagine.

Andy thanked the chef and politely refused. His stomach had begun to flip-flop all over the place as the reality of his situation had fully dawned on him.

I couldn't eat even if I wanted to, Andy thought. *I'm too nervous.*

Andy settled himself in his seat and stared out a brass porthole, watching the earth below him gently recede. His right hand rested on a leather-bound mission briefing his grandfather had given him. With his left hand, he tightly held the Hodges Zoomwriter.

Ned had told him that the journey to the tropics would take several days and that he should try to make himself comfortable. As he looked around, he didn't think getting comfortable would be difficult.

Andy looked out the window again. The ground was moving farther and farther away. Turning his attention to the mission briefing in front of him, he opened the file. The symbol of the Jungle Explorers' Society was printed on the first page.

This is amazing. It's like being a secret agent!

Curious, Andy began to read:

DEAR GRANDSON,

THE MISSION YOU ARE UNDERTAKING IS OF THE utmost IMPORTANCE TO THE SAFETY AND SECURITY of the entire world. It is but the first of several adventures that I shall be imploring you to help me upon.

YEARS AGO, I WAS TASKED WITH PROTECTING A SERIES OF MAGICAL ARTIFACTS AND ENSURING THAT THEY ARE KEPT HIDDEN FROM THE REST OF THE WORLD. THESE ANCIENT TREASURED ITEMS ARE VALUED ABOVE MEASURE, EACH BEING IMBUED WITH UNUSUAL POWERS.

It is to my great embarrassment and dismay that enemies of the Society have learned the locations of some of these treasures and are trying to find and use them for their own nefarious purposes.

I have a guess as to who might be behind the foul plot. The villain's name is almost too terrible to mention, for merely hearing it has caused many who have had the misfortune of meeting him to tremble.

Suffice it to say, this horrible man calls

himself Professor Phink. He has been my adversary in all I've set out to do in my illustrious career. He is, I suspect, the one who arranged for my capture by the witch doctor who shrank my head.

The funeral you attended was arranged to throw Phink off the scent. If he believes me dead, we may have a chance to catch him unaware and keep him from retrieving the artifacts.

Of the many objects I have been tasked with protecting, none is more powerful than the Pailina Pendant. This is what I believe Phink seeks. I am trusting you to keep it out of his hands. You are, in fact, the only one I can trust. But to keep it from him, you must first find a key that can unlock the hidden chamber in which the pendant is hidden.

By the time you read this, the villainous Professor Phink may well have become aware of your departure, for he has eyes and ears everywhere. If he finds the key before we do, the fate of the entire world may be at stake. The power it unlocks would bring disaster on a scale never before seen, and many innocent lives would surely be lost.

Stay vigilant and keep your pen at hand! Phink will stop at nothing to thwart those who interfere with his plans, but in this case, the pen is indeed mightier than the sword. Ha!

You'll be landing in a few days at the Society's hidden Hawaiian headquarters. There you will rendezvous with my friend and associate Albert Awol. He will give you additional information and equip you with the supplies needed to complete your mission.

Enjoy your first adventure! And if you get nervous, here is a simple cure: stand on your head and recite the alphabet backward three times as rapidly as possible. When you stand upright again, you'll find that you've completely forgotten whatever it was that was bothering you and have a pleasant dizzy feeling as well.

Godspeed to you, Grandson! I only wish I were thirty years younger and could join you on this exciting expedition.

Kungaloosh!

Grandfather

Behind the letter was a drawing of a tiki. It looked like one of the carved gods he'd seen in books about Polynesia, except it was pocket-sized and placed on the handle of an ornately carved wooden key. Beneath it were the words TIKI KEY.

"Strange," Andy muttered.

Turning the pages of the file, Andy saw maps of Hawaii and the surrounding islands.

As he closed the file, a feeling of resolve washed over him. If what his grandfather had said was true, then the fate of the world might indeed be resting on his shoulders. He straightened in his seat, removed the small leather notebook his grandfather had given him, twisted the cap on his pen, and wrote:

Read the briefing. Will do my best.

He hesitated, then added to the transmission the parting phrase his grandfather liked to use.

Kungaloosh!

Chapter Seven
Professor Phink

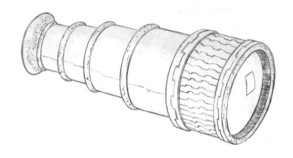

His eyes were yellow. They were the first thing people noticed about him and the last thing his victims saw.

Their particular hue was not a beautiful gold but was instead reminiscent of something pestilent. The whites of his eyes were also yellow, creating a macabre look. Anyone who made eye contact with him tended to look away immediately, a welcome reaction in his line of work.

His eyes stood in stark contrast to the rest of him, all of which was cloaked in black. His ebony hair was plastered neatly away from his high, pale brow, and a rather diabolical pencil-thin mustache crept along his upper lip.

From his perch on the edge of a wall at the Lostmore mansion, he watched the ascent of Ned Lostmore's zeppelin with interest. He was especially intrigued by the young passenger he'd seen escorted onto the vessel. The wall he sat on provided adequate cover for his spying and had been frequented by the professor on many previous occasions. He had, in fact, sat there mere hours earlier to watch the events of Ned's funeral unfold. He hadn't believed for a second that the burial ceremony he'd witnessed was authentic. It had too much of his adversary's style about it, which could only mean that somehow—against impossible odds—Ned Lostmore had survived his encounter with the witch doctor Phink had hired to shrink his head.

Folding up his spyglass, Professor Phink turned his

attention to a small shadowy figure beside him.

"Our plan must not fail," he said in his rich, sonorous voice. "Remember to stick closely to it. I cannot afford to have anything go awry. The Potentate has special plans for the Pailina Pendant, and she doesn't take kindly to failure. Do you understand?"

The figure next to him glanced up, her eyes crinkling as she smiled.

"Of course," she said.

Abigail Awol was as different in appearance from the professor as was possible. Strikingly beautiful, with neatly coiffed hair, full ruby lips, and dark, expressive eyes, she was petite, standing a mere five feet tall.

The girl was a strong ally, but Phink was not foolish enough to share the entirety of his plan with her. She had too much conscience, though she tried to hide it. But for jobs she didn't need to know all the details of, Abigail was perfect. It was she who had arranged to have Ned's head shrunk.

With Ned out of the way, Phink's plan should have

proceeded like clockwork. The artifacts Lostmore had been guarding should have been left unprotected and easily procured.

So why was Ned's zeppelin headed skyward? Where was it bound, and had Ned Lostmore found some way to orchestrate a last-minute plan to stop him from achieving his goal?

If so, he's a fool, the professor mused. Hadn't he always been one step ahead of that bumbling doctor and his ridiculous cures?

Phink turned his cruel gaze back down to his agent.

"I want to know who is on board before you shoot it down. Is that understood?" he snapped.

"Perfectly," Abigail replied.

Then, flashing him her beautiful smile, she disappeared into the shadows.

Chapter Eight
A Rude Awakening

Aboard the zeppelin, Andy soon found himself unable to keep his eyes open. Before long, the light drone of the zeppelin's engines had lulled him to sleep.

The next few days of travel passed surprisingly quickly. Andy found that the zeppelin had been fitted with plenty of clean clothing, and its library had been stocked not only with all his grandfather's books, but with hundreds of books about Polynesian history, mythology, and geography, which he happily settled in to read.

Andy began with Ned's book *Witch Doctors: A Prescription for Madness?* He had read it before, but now that he was on an adventure of his own, it was even more exciting to read Ned's firsthand account of the challenges he'd faced while going up against mysterious jungle magic.

When he had reread all of Ned's books, Andy moved on to a series of books in the zeppelin's library that were devoted to Hawaiian culture and history.

Might as well do some light research before I get there.

By the fourth day of the journey, Andy was feeling well versed in the history of Hawaii. He was immersed in a new book about the geography of Molokai when a loud bang interrupted his reading.

What was that?

Andy looked around the cockpit, confused and a

little alarmed. He'd gotten so comfortable in the airship over the past few days that sometimes it was easy to forget he was suspended above the earth in a motorized balloon.

Andy moved to one of the brass portholes and stared out. There was something flying next to him.

"A biplane?" he murmured. He stared at the double-winged plane. It had a military insignia on it, but Andy couldn't place the country it was from. "German, maybe?" he wondered. "No. Looks more like—"

The blimp lurched violently to the side as several bullets tore through the cabin, exploding into the cabinets behind him.

Andy covered his head with his hands, cowering behind the sofa. When the shooting stopped, he peeked over the couch just in time to see the biplane zoom past the cabin window.

"We're under attack!" he shouted.

Andy stumbled toward the cockpit, aware of the roar of the biplane's engines outside. The ship rocked from side to side, and the wind howled through the perforated cabin, scattering papers and throwing everything into disarray.

Andy ripped open the door to the cockpit.

"There's a plane shooting at us!" he shouted. "There's a—" The words died in his throat. The pilot's seat was empty! Worse still, Andy saw that the airship was plunging toward the ocean. Through the windshield he could just make out the tops of two brightly colored parachutes. With a sinking sensation, he realized why he hadn't heard any other panicked voices on the zeppelin. The crew had bailed out and left him behind!

The zeppelin shook as another round of bullets tore through its hull. Andy heard a loud *THUNK! THUNK! THUNK!* as the shells slammed into the engines. A second later, the steady thrum of the propellers stopped and an eerie silence overtook the ship.

A tremendous explosion came from behind him, and Andy was hurled toward the pilot's seat.

He caught himself on the seat and stood, staring out

the windshield at the approaching water beneath him. Out of the corner of his eye, he saw the biplane pilot lean out of the cockpit. He turned toward her grinning face as she saluted him.

Andy shook his head. *I've got to find a way out!* He glanced around the cabin and noticed an emergency exit. In a flash, he realized that the pilot must have used that door to get out at the first sign of danger.

As the biplane receded in the distance, the full horror of Andy's situation struck him. If he didn't do something fast, the zeppelin was going to end up at the bottom of the ocean—with him inside!

Andy wanted to scream, but he knew his best chance at survival was to remain calm. He rushed back into the cabin. Throwing open cabinets and doors, he searched for anything he could use.

Finally, he spotted something. On a high shelf was a parachute.

Andy grabbed it and strapped it on. *This had better work,* he thought, racing back to the cockpit. *I don't even know if I'm wearing it right!* He leapt for the emergency exit and turned the handle. It didn't budge. *Locked! What am I going to—*

Suddenly, Andy remembered the key ring at his belt. *The skeleton key! Of course!*

Andy grabbed the ring and shoved the rusty key into the lock. *Come on!* He grunted as he turned the key, twisting it with all his might. The lock was stubborn, but finally it gave way and the door flew open.

Thank you, Grandfather!

The wind roared in his ears, and the ocean surged below him. A second blast ripped through the ship as the other engine exploded in a ball of flame.

There was no time to think, no time to consider the fact that he'd never used a parachute before. Andy hesitated only a moment as he gripped the sides of the doorframe, and then, with his heart in his throat, he jumped.

Chapter Nine
Splash Landing

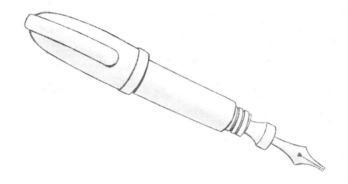

A ndy tumbled through the air. He felt like he was in the middle of a hurricane. His heart pounded faster than it ever had before, and it was all he could do to stay clearheaded instead of screaming.

Why isn't my chute opening? It's supposed to open!

Tears were pulled from the corners of his eyes, and the forceful winds continued to howl around his body as he fell farther and farther—faster and faster.

Something's wrong!

Then, in a flash, he remembered that to deploy the chute, the handle on the pack had to be pulled.

He cursed quietly to himself for forgetting such an obvious thing and frantically patted the straps around his chest, searching for the metal handle. For a moment, he thought it wasn't there, and a new wave of panic rushed over him. But his desperately probing fingers soon found what he was looking for, and he jerked on the metal ring as hard as he could.

He felt the release of the folded nylon as it shot out of the pack.

FOOMP!

The parachute blossomed above him, and his fall was cut short with a hard, snapping jerk.

Seconds later he was gazing down, searching for a safe place to land.

But there was no land. There was nothing but ocean in every direction.

When he'd seen pictures of parachutes in books, the

descent had always looked peaceful—more like floating than falling—but the reality was quite different. The parachute had slowed his fall, but Andy was surprised at how quickly he was still moving.

He hit the surface of the water with a tremendous splash, then plunged down, down, down into the icy depths, like a knife through butter. He was farther down than he'd ever been before in the murky depths of the ocean. His lungs screamed for air as he tried to paddle back to the surface.

Andy's fear of drowning propelled his arms upward through the icy water. He ignored the ache in his shoulders and back, telling himself over and over, *I can do this. I'm not going to drown. I can do this!*

In a last desperate lunge, Andy burst from the surface, sputtering, coughing, and taking deep, shuddering gasps of air.

His lips were trembling with cold, and he knew by the stiffness in his arms and legs that he didn't have much time before his strength gave out.

Andy gazed around, panicked. *There are no ships. No anything!*

The thought of drowning at sea hadn't occurred to him when he agreed to go on this mission. But now it was becoming an increasingly likely reality!

Don't panic! he told himself. *Panicking will only make things worse. You'll use too much energy trying to stay afloat!*

But he *was* panicking. A small wave crashed over his head, and he sputtered and coughed through chattering teeth.

Before he could take a second breath, another icy wave broke over Andy's head, pushing him back below the surface. It took all his strength to paddle upward again and tread water.

"Help!" Andy shouted. But even as he called, he knew it was useless. There was nobody around for miles.

Andy's aching arms slowed their desperate treading.

I can't... can't keep this up.

His mind raced with fear.

I'm going to drown here. No one will ever know what happened to me. I'll just disappear. . . .

Andy felt the water inch up toward his nose. Then, suddenly, an idea hit him.

The Zoomwriter!

The thought was like being thrown a life preserver.

Andy fumbled in his trouser pockets, his numb fingers clutching at anything they found there. To his profound relief, he felt them brush against the barrel of the pen. He withdrew it from his pocket and moved the cap to the back. Then, with his last ounce of strength, he pushed down hard three times on the cap.

Grandfather said that help would come. And it will, Andy told himself, trying to draw hope from the words. Struggling to keep his head above the water, Andy searched for the promised help.

Someone . . . please!

But as the seconds ticked by, any hope the pen had provided him with gave way to despair. Rescue was impossible. He had no idea where he was, and even if the pen had transmitted a distress signal, how in the world could his grandfather get anyone to him in time?

Andy's arms and legs were numb. He'd expended every bit of effort he could manage. His heart felt like lead as he realized that his last moments on Earth were rapidly disappearing.

With an unexpected calm, Andy Stanley allowed himself to sink slowly below the surface and resigned himself to the fate that awaited him in the briny deep.

Good-bye, Grandfather. I'm so sorry I failed you....

Chapter Ten
Hoku

A ndy awoke to find himself lying on a cot, a beak hovering near his nose. He would have jumped backward in shock, but he found that his arms and legs were so sore he could barely move.

"You're up. He's up!" A cockatiel hopped excitedly on Andy's chest.

A second voice chimed in from behind the cot where Andy lay.

"Keep it down, Hoku! The kid needs rest."

The bird—who Andy assumed was Hoku—bobbed her plumed head, still excited. She tried to lower her voice, but it came out in a hoarse, excited whisper. "You've been through a lot, Andy Stanley. You're lucky we found you, yes you are." Then, as if whispering were too difficult to manage for more than a few seconds, the bird called out in a loud voice, "He's lucky we found him, isn't he? Isn't he, Skipper?"

"Yes, Hoku, you dumb bird. He's lucky. Now what part of *quiet* didn't you understand?" said a man, coming into view. Andy noticed that the man was carrying a bamboo tray loaded with a Brown Betty teapot and three slightly cracked cups. He could only assume the man was the "skipper" to whom the bird was speaking.

Hoku, who was still perched on Andy's chest, dipped her head and looked shamefaced. "Sorry, Skip." Then she forced her voice into a loud whisper again and looked back at Andy. "Sorry!"

Andy stared at the bird, dumbfounded. Thoughts

like *What happened?*, *How did I get here?*, and *Did that bird actually talk?* swirled around his aching head.

"Who are you? And how did you get her to do that?" he croaked at the strange man. "Is it some kind of trick?"

Hoku fluffed out her feathers in irritation, and she squawked loudly. The man guffawed. "Oh, you shouldn't have said that, boy. You don't want to make an enemy of old Hoku," he said. "She hates being compared to . . . what shall we call them . . . *ordinary* birds."

Andy winced as he pushed himself up on his elbows. Hoku had flown to a nearby window and was staring outside. Andy got the impression that she was offended and trying to ignore him.

"I'm sorry, Hoku. I didn't know. I . . . I've never met anything quite like you before," he said.

Hoku preened for a moment, then seemed to decide that Andy's apology was sufficient. Hopping down from the window, she fluttered to sit on the man's shoulder.

The big man chuckled, his eyes twinkling. "Aw, see there? She's decided to forgive you." He tickled the bird under the chin.

Andy studied the man in front of him, noting his grizzled appearance. He was tall, and his head nearly touched the rafters. His rumpled shirt showed signs of serious wear, and he wore mismatched socks beneath a pair of grimy Bermuda shorts.

Andy suddenly felt self-conscious. He realized that he didn't know where he was or who this person who had apparently come to his rescue was.

"Um, excuse me. You seem to know my name, but I still don't know yours," he said. "Who are you, if you don't mind my asking? And where am I?"

The man replied in a deep, resonant voice. "Albert Awol, onetime skipper and known to most of my listeners as the Voice of the Jungle. I run a small radio station out of my hut here."

Albert gestured expansively to the slightly cluttered room. Andy noticed a small desk, a microphone, and a very old record player surrounded by shelves of carefully stacked records.

"And you've already met Hoku. She's just one of several enchanted birds that occupy the Tiki Room, not far from here. As to where you are, you're in Hawaii."

Albert handed Andy a cup of warm tea.

Andy took a sip and felt immediately comforted. The tea had a wonderful blend of flavors he'd never encountered before, something tropical, with the scent of hibiscus flowers.

"The Tiki Room? What is that?" Andy asked.

"It's a magical place," Albert answered. "Ancient. Only people invited there are allowed entrance.

"Your grandfather discovered the Tiki Room on one of his expeditions," Albert continued. "He was looking for a magic feather that was rumored to give whoever found it the ability to fly!"

At the mention of his grandfather, something stirred in the back of Andy's mind. "Albert Awol," he said, rolling the name around in his head. "My grandfather said I was supposed to find you. Of course, I didn't expect you to be rescuing me from a zeppelin crash."

Albert laughed. "I knew you were coming and didn't expect that, either. Your grandfather is one of my closest friends. There's nobody who knows more about jungle exploration and exotic cures. He cured Hoku of a terrible case of the Amazonian jungle flu."

Hoku nodded enthusiastically. "He did, he did! Great man, your grandfather. A great man!"

Albert continued, "We picked up the distress call he sent, but even hopping right on *Annie*, I barely got to you in time."

"Annie?" Andy asked, puzzled.

"*Amazon Annie*, my jungle boat. That old gal and I have had some mighty fun adventures together," Albert explained. "Rushed her to you as fast as I could. Just managed to pull you out of the drink. Saw the wreckage. You're lucky you survived!"

So the pen had worked after all. Andy felt around in his pockets and was relieved to find that the Zoomwriter was still there. His grandfather had been right about how important it was. If he hadn't remembered it, he certainly would have drowned!

"You saved my life," Andy said. "I don't know how to thank you. . . ."

Albert shrugged. "Don't thank me. Thank Madame Wiki. She's the medicine woman who cured your hypothermia."

Hoku hopped up and down, excited. "She is the keeper of the Tiki Room. She knows about the old magic, she does. Very old magic."

"Madame Wiki?" Andy asked, interested. "Where is she? My grandfather said that I was supposed to find something called the . . . Tiki Key. Do you think she might know about it?"

Albert scratched his stubbly chin. "Oh yes. She's been part of the Society for a long time. But you're in no condition to go see her yet. You need to rest."

Albert grabbed a pith helmet from a nearby hat rack and then put on a heavy canvas jacket. "Hoku will look after you," he said. "I've got an appointment with Trader Sam . . . a world traveler with a good head for business. He's only here for one day, and he's supposed to do an interview on my show this afternoon."

Albert pointed a thick finger at Andy. "If you're anything like your grandfather, you're probably itching to get on with your mission. Don't wander off. The Molokai jungle is no place to go exploring without a guide."

Andy nodded. He'd read enough about the tropics to know that dangerous animals and venomous insects could be lurking anywhere. He would rather have a guide than stumble into something horrible unawares.

Andy reached into his pocket and wrapped his fingers around the Zoomwriter. He might need it soon.

With a last nod at Andy, Albert walked out of the hut.

Andy waited until he was sure Albert was gone, and then he carefully swung his legs over the edge of the cot. Wincing at his incredibly sore muscles, he eased himself off the bed.

"Careful, Andy Stanley. Be careful!" said Hoku.

"Albert says you should rest, yes, you should. Rest is what you should do."

Andy ignored the bird. He was too curious about his new surroundings. If he was indeed going to be there for a while, he might as well make the most of his time.

Someone tried to kill me. And now here I am, stuck in a stranger's hut. He says his name is Albert Awol, but how do I know he's telling the truth? He could be anyone! I need to find out more about him.

Andy limped across the room, navigating carefully around the assorted bric-a-brac that filled Albert's hut. He noted a piece of an airplane wing, an African spear, several cracked teapots, and some big band sheet music. On a rickety coffee table was a book of Hawaiian mythology. Andy leafed through it, taking note of the vivid illustrations of various Hawaiian gods and goddesses.

Koro, the midnight dancer; Pele, goddess of fire and volcanoes; Maui, the mighty one; Ngendei, the earth balancer . . . Boy, there are a lot of them!

Andy would have loved nothing more than to pore

over the book with another cup of that delicious tea, but it was not the time. He replaced it on the table. *Maybe I'll have a chance to read it later. Some extra information on Hawaiian culture might come in handy.*

Across the room, Andy spotted a shelf containing a number of framed photographs. Moving slowly so as to avoid another injury, he hobbled to the shelf.

Andy picked up the first photo. It was a picture of Albert with two people Andy assumed were his wife and daughter. Albert looked much younger in the photo than the man Andy had just met, and Andy recognized him as the man in the photo at Ned's house. The three were standing in front of an old-fashioned biplane with the words JUNGLE NAVIGATION COMPANY scrawled across the fuselage in curling script.

Andy studied the photo. The girl was very pretty. *Wow, what a beautiful smile*, he thought. *There's something familiar about her. Where have I seen her before?*

Andy set the picture back on the shelf and made his way down the row of photos. A good many showed an older Albert than the first photo. *That's odd. Albert is alone in most of these. I wonder what happened to his wife and daughter. Why were there no more pictures of them?*

Andy's gaze wandered lazily over the next few photos. When he reached the last picture in the row, his eyes widened in surprise. In his eagerness, he grabbed the frame.

It was a much younger version of Albert with another boy about his own age.

If Andy hadn't known better, he would have sworn that he was looking at a picture of himself. The boy in the picture was tall and thin, with the same pale complexion and straw-like sandy hair. Both boys were wearing safari gear, and they stood arm in arm, grinning broadly.

Andy turned the photograph over and saw that there was something written on the back of the frame.

ALBERT AND NED ON THEIR FIRST EXPEDITION.

"Grandfather," Andy breathed.

A voice behind him made him jump.

"My best friend," Albert Awol said.

Chapter Eleven
The Villains

Andy turned and saw Albert standing in the doorway. He suddenly felt self-conscious for snooping around the skipper's hut.

"I was just . . . I mean, I'm sorry if I . . ." Andy stammered.

Albert waved him off. "Wouldn't have expected anything less from Ned's grandson. In fact, I'd have done the same thing."

He walked over to Andy. "Forgot my bug repellent,"

Albert said with a shrug. He took the framed photo from Andy's hand and smiled.

"Ned and I couldn't be separated at that age. We were both determined to join the Jungle Explorers' Society. Of course, Ned was the one approached first for membership. They'd been watching him for years."

Albert's gaze grew distant as he stared at the old photo. A strange look passed over his face. He seemed to be contemplating something deeply.

"When we were boys, Ned was always coming in first in everything. He had the highest marks at school; teachers and classmates adored him. . . . You get the idea." Albert chuckled. "Quite the hero, your grandfather. But he was also kind enough to vouch for me to the Society. That picture was taken just after we were accepted. It was the proudest day of our lives. We'd spent hours studying explorers. We'd memorized every map we could get our hands on and even made a few of our own. Those were happy times."

Albert handed the photo back to Andy, who peered

at it again. *I guess that answers that. Albert must be who he says he is. This photo proves it.*

Andy set the photo down and looked back at Albert.

"When I heard about his encounter with the head shrinker, I couldn't believe my ears," Albert said. "The great Ned Lostmore outsmarted by a witch doctor? Nonsense!" Albert waved his hand wildly. "And when Cedric wrote to me about the upcoming funeral, I was devastated. I wanted to attend but was detained here due to a tropical storm." Albert sighed and shook his head. "Hard to imagine a world without Ned in it. Thank goodness it was just an elaborate ploy."

He laughed and waved his hand again in a dismissive gesture. "That ceremony was classic Ned, doing everything he could to throw them off his scent. But I can't believe that he actually had his head shrunk. Such bad luck, there."

"Excuse me," Andy interrupted. "But who do you mean by 'them'? Was it Professor Phink's henchman who shot down the zeppelin, or was it someone else?"

Andy shifted on his feet nervously. "My grandfather mentioned that he had many enemies."

Albert looked Andy over, as if sizing him up. "If your grandfather didn't tell you, then maybe I shouldn't—"

"Please," Andy begged. "This whole adventure is already much more than I ever wanted. If I don't know anything about my adversaries, I think I'll go crazy. I can't stand to be constantly looking over my shoulder and wondering if someone is going to . . ."

"Stab you in the back?" Albert finished.

Feeling pained, Andy nodded in agreement.

"Well, I do know something about being betrayed," Albert replied. He moved to the shelf and removed the photograph that Andy had examined earlier.

Hoku fluttered to Albert's shoulder, looking agitated. Albert stroked the bird's feathers, murmuring soothingly to her. Then he pointed to the young girl in the photo.

"I taught my daughter, Abigail, everything I know. How to pilot a plane, skipper a boat, navigate through jungles, and be an expert in self-defense. Ned always said she would be the best of us, that she would probably be the head of our society one day. I wanted her to continue the legacy. . . ."

Albert's eyes became misty. "We were a close family. But when her mother died, something changed in her. She blamed me for the accident that took her mother's life. After that, nothing was ever the same between us."

Andy didn't know what to say. He could tell that the memories were terribly painful for Albert, but he was at a loss as to how to help. After a long silence he asked in a small voice, "What happened?"

Albert sighed and shook his head. "Exploring the temple was your grandfather's idea. He said the Society had gotten an anonymous tip that there was a rare specimen of plant in the area. Ned could never resist the possibility of finding a new cure, and he was sure the leaves had extraordinary healing properties, in spite of all the stories about a curse."

Albert waved his gnarled hand. "Nothing new, really. Ned has always ignored danger when he is really intent upon a discovery. Laughed it off with one of his silly jokes."

"He does have an interesting sense of humor," Andy confessed.

Albert snorted. "I'll say," he grumbled. "But there's a brilliant mind behind those jests. Your grandfather was . . . *is* . . . an amazing man."

Andy noticed how Albert corrected himself. He had to admit that if he hadn't seen his grandfather's condition for himself, he wouldn't have known how to describe Ned's current state, either.

Albert looked back at the picture of his wife and daughter. "Lucy wanted to go with me. She said that I'd been gone too much and that we needed more family time together. Abigail, of course, was dying to go. It was going to be her first real adventure, and we'd been training together for so long."

Albert brushed a hand across his teary eyes.

"I should have said no," Albert continued in a broken voice. "Shouldn't have even gone myself. I knew the temple was dangerous, but I never thought that our enemies would arrange an ambush.

"They knew that Ned was Keymaster and figured that by capturing him they could make him give up the secret locations of the treasures we were entrusted to protect. But they didn't know him like we do. Ned would never betray us."

Albert sighed. "Lucy . . . died in the attack. . . . No matter how I tried to convince Abigail that the professor wasn't who he said he was, that he was working for our enemies, she still believed the ambush was my fault. Ned and I knew the professor from our days at university. He always wanted to be a part of the Jungle Explorers' Society, but they saw through him. They knew he was a bad egg. Everyone did."

"The professor?" Andy asked. "You mean Phink? What can you tell me about him?"

Albert fixed Andy with a steely gaze. "Professor Phink is the opposite of your grandfather in every way possible. He's unlike anyone in the Society. We are tasked with finding and protecting powerful objects. Phink just wants to find them and use them for his own gain. He's diabolical. If he gets his hands on the artifacts, well, let's just say I don't think the world as we know it will exist anymore."

Albert's voice broke again and he looked away. "Phink lied to Abigail about me. He knew she had talent. She's . . . she's working for him now." Albert turned his gaze from Andy and stared out the window. "She ran away before I could tell her how sorry I was. I would give anything to tell her how much I love her."

Andy stared at the photograph of the smiling girl. Suddenly, he knew where he'd seen that smile before.

It's the pilot who shot down the zeppelin!

Andy looked at Albert, unsure whether he should mention the incident. What did it matter? He could see that the man's heart was broken over the loss of his daughter. Telling him that she'd nearly killed Andy wouldn't solve anything.

Andy's thoughts wandered to Professor Phink. If he

was indeed the one behind the zeppelin attack, then he would likely resort to any means necessary to keep Andy from finding what he was supposed to protect. For the first time, Andy realized how important it was for him to complete his quest.

"Mr. Awol, if this person is as dangerous as you say he is, then I'd better find that Tiki Key as soon as possible," Andy said.

"Are you sure that you're up to it?" Albert asked.

Andy nodded. "I'm a little sore, but I can handle it."

Albert rested a big hand on Andy's shoulder. "Your grandfather would be proud of you, son." Then he turned to Hoku and gave the bird a serious look. "You know what to do," he said.

Hoku bobbed her head and flapped over to Andy's shoulder. "Follow me close," she said. "Close. Follow. Follow me close."

Andy nodded. Hoku seemed about to fly away, but then she turned to Andy and fixed him with an intense gaze.

"Follow close, Andy, follow close. Follow Hoku, or you will die."

With that, she flew from Andy's shoulder toward the door. Andy followed as fast as his legs could carry him.

Chapter Twelve
A Dangerous Situation

The path Hoku led Andy down was littered with twisting roots and vines that seemed almost to reach out and grab at his shoes, causing him to trip. Andy soon found himself covered with scrapes from falling down and skinning his knees.

"Ow! Wait up, will you?" he shouted as a particularly

large vine sent him sprawling into a mass of thorny jungle plants.

Hearing his cry, Hoku fluttered to a nearby branch to examine his latest injury.

"Not bad, not bad," she chirped. "Could be worse. Ned's grandson is a clumsy one, isn't he? Not so much like his grandfather, is he? No, not so much."

Andy glowered at Hoku. "I never said I was like him," he replied. He stood up and brushed off his knees. "How much farther do we have to go?"

"The Tiki Room is not far," Hoku said. "Easy for birds, but hard for boys, yes . . . difficult for you but not for Hoku. But getting inside will be dangerous. Very dangerous. Must not anger the tikis, Andy Stanley. No, no, must not!"

The tikis? Andy thought. Until then he'd thought of the Hawaiian gods only as elaborately carved wooden statues. How could they be angered?

As Hoku set off again and Andy followed, he decided not to bring it up. He figured the best answer he'd get from Hoku would probably be to wait and see.

And she'll probably repeat herself a dozen times when she says it, Andy thought. He'd already grown used to the idea that a bird could hold a conversation, and the novelty had worn off. Now Hoku was irritating him. She talked to him like he was stupid.

After several more minutes of stumbling through the dense jungle growth, a very scratched-up Andy emerged in a clearing. In the center stood a quaint Polynesian hut with a thatched roof.

Would you look at that! Andy mused.

The pitch of the roof was very steep, and Andy could tell that it had been constructed meticulously. Exotic lamps and painted fabric with swirling Polynesian figures decorated the exterior. Flanking the entrance to the hut were two pillars, the images of grinning tribal shields, their long tongues sticking out, carved into the columns.

They almost look friendly, Andy thought. But there was something about the carvings that seemed mystical, like they were guarding an ancient place of great significance.

A bamboo fence surrounded the grounds. Andy noticed several more carved figures in the tall grass leading up to the entrance.

The statues cast an aura of mystery around the sacred place. Andy couldn't decide whether he wanted to go in or go away. There was something calming about the hut, but nothing having to do with Ned was easy, and Andy was sure there was probably much more danger surrounding the Tiki Room than appeared at first glance.

Hoku hopped down from a nearby branch onto Andy's shoulder. She preened her feathers for a bit. "Proceed with caution, boy. Caution, boy, caution," she said. "Do not anger the tikis!"

"They're made of stone and wood," Andy protested. "How can I anger them? By accidentally knocking them over?"

Hoku fixed him with a beady eye. "No joke, Andy Stanley. Not a joke! You must tread carefully. Carefully!

There are many traps, many hurtful traps that can snare careless, clumsy boys."

Andy resented Hoku for pointing out that he was clumsy. Maybe he was, but he didn't need someone he had just met reminding him of it. He felt a wave of irritation rise inside him as he stared at the field with the scattered tikis. From what he could see, there was nothing to make him suspect a trap of any kind. Eager to prove Hoku wrong, he marched determinedly toward the statues.

"Beware, beware!" Hoku squawked.

As he drew close to the first statue, Andy felt a strange, almost magnetic pull. He was surprised when the little hairs on the back of his neck and arms slowly rose. He looked at the statue's vague, expressionless eyes.

Suddenly, clouds obscured the sun and there was a crack of distant thunder. Andy's feet became rooted to the ground. Try as he might, he couldn't move them an inch. With a sense of rising panic, he struggled to get free, but he was stuck as tightly as a fly on flypaper. *What's happening? I... I can't move!*

Just then, a deep feminine voice echoed around him.

"Bow before me, mortal!" the voice boomed.

Andy felt his knees buckle. His eyes grew wide with terror and he gazed around, trying to determine the source of the voice.

"Who's there?" Andy asked. But he was so scared his voice was a tiny squeak.

An invisible force like a giant hand pressed him down into a kneeling position in the soft earth. Thunder shook the ground, and Andy heard a loud cracking noise. He looked around in horror as deep cracks opened up in the earth, exposing rivers of molten lava that rose higher and higher from some unfathomable depth below.

"What is my name?" the voice thundered.

Perhaps it was because he was panicked, but Andy was confused by the question. *I don't know what she means. How could I possibly know her name? It's not a fair question!*

He could smell clouds of burning sulfur rising from the rapidly spreading cracks. From somewhere to the east a hot wind began to blow, riffling Andy's blond hair and bringing with it a terrifying sense of mounting catastrophe.

I didn't sign up for this! I'm . . . I'm not prepared!

"Hoku!" Andy screamed.

The bird was nowhere to be seen. In fact, the smoldering vapors were stinging Andy's eyes, making it nearly impossible to see much of *anything* around him.

Andy struggled to free his knees from the earth. *Think, Andy, think! There's got to be a rational explanation for all this!*

But Andy couldn't think of one. The situation he found himself in defied logic. It felt as if the Earth's gravity were working against him.

The hot lava had risen higher in the cracks. Andy could feel the searing heat radiating from the molten rock. It burned his cheeks, and he knew if he didn't do something soon, he would be overwhelmed by the encroaching lava.

A stone the size of a soccer ball burst into flame, and Andy nearly screamed. He had to calm down. He would never get out of this situation if he just sat there hyperventilating.

He tried to calm his rapid breathing. "Okay, think. Maybe there are clues that could help me answer her question," he murmured. "If we're dealing with tikis, then the only logical explanation is that the voice is supposed to belong to some kind of goddess."

Andy racked his brain for an answer, turning over anything that might trigger a connection.

Another crack of thunder split the air. The heat and sulfurous fumes were making Andy feel light-headed.

Think!

Andy gazed at the storm clouds that roiled above him. He glanced at the flaming stone that glowed with intense heat near his feet.

It's so hot that it's practically melting! It's turning into lava....

And then, suddenly, he had it. He knew the answer to the question the voice had asked. He had seen it in the book on Albert's table, the one about Hawaiian mythology!

But in trying to answer, he let out a series of coughs instead.

With a thin voice, strained to the point of breaking from the fumes, he answered, "You're Pele!" And then he added, "The . . . g-goddess of fire and volcanoes."

As suddenly as it had come, the heavy force that had pinned him to the earth lifted. The cracks in the ground around him rumbled to a close, and the winds died down. Within moments, the world around him had been restored to its previous, tranquil state.

Andy got up and looked directly at the carved effigy of the Hawaiian goddess that stood a few feet in front of him. It stared back at him, as lifeless as it had seemed before. Evidently, Andy had answered correctly, because the thundering voice didn't speak again.

Somewhere above him, a bird chirped. Andy heard a flapping next to his ear and felt Hoku settle on his shoulder. He looked reproachfully at the bird, angry that she had deserted him when he'd been so close to death.

"Decided to come back?" he snapped irritably.

Hoku glanced at him. "I warned you, boy. Warned you, I did. But you ran off and didn't listen, no. No, the boy didn't listen!" Hoku replied.

Andy looked away. He didn't want to admit that she had a point. He hadn't taken the danger seriously, and it had nearly killed him.

"Sorry," he mumbled. "I didn't realize. . . ."

"Apology—*awk!*—accepted," Hoku squawked cheerily. "Now Andy knows, knows he does. Traps all around and very dangerous. Danger, danger, dangerous!"

"Yeah, 'danger, danger, dangerous.' I understand," Andy said. "But what I don't understand is how I was forced to the ground and how the ground opened and closed so quickly. I couldn't move! It's not scientifically possible!"

Hoku gave him another of her piercing stares. "Didn't Grandfather tell you? Grandfather didn't tell you, boy? He didn't tell you?"

"Tell me what?" Andy asked. But as the words left his mouth, he remembered what his grandfather had said when they'd first met. He recalled Ned's serious expression and the glint on his monocle as he'd replied to Andy's question about the impossibility of his grandfather's new, shrunken-headed existence. Andy hadn't known what to make of it at the time, but now the answer came back with more force and relevance than before.

"There are many types of magic in the jungle, some more mysterious than science can readily supply us answers to," Andy murmured. "Wow. I guess he was right after all."

Chapter Thirteen
Treading Carefully

Having experienced for himself what the tikis
could do, Andy made a mental note to tread more
carefully going forward. He could see four more statues
remaining between him and the door of the hut. The
way between them had a clearly worn path.

Andy walked along the narrow trail, praying that

his clumsiness wouldn't surface. He could only imagine what might happen if he bumped into one of the wooden effigies—or, worse, knocked one over!

Andy's every step was slow and focused, and soon sweat was beading on his forehead from the effort not to trip. But often the harder one concentrates on not doing something, the more likely it is to happen.

Andy was so intent on avoiding the gnarled tree branches that he didn't see a small stone in his path. The toe of his brown boot slipped on the pebble, and he flew forward.

Hoku, caught by surprise, let out a terrified squawk and flapped from Andy's narrow shoulder.

"Whoa, whoa, whoa!" Andy yelled. His arms windmilled like crazy as he tried to find his balance.

Despite his best efforts, Andy smashed into a tiki. The name NGENDEI was carved into a small wooden sign next to it. As he collided with the wooden effigy, a booming voice filled the air, howling with rage. There was an almost impossibly bright flash and a crack that

Andy thought was thunder. But the disaster wasn't over yet. As Ngendei toppled, Andy's legs went with it, and he rolled down the short slope that led to the other tikis. He crashed into them and they fell to the ground.

"*Aaah, ow! Agh!*" Andy screamed. His heart pounded with dread. He'd desecrated the sacred grounds! *They're not going to like that!*

A loud crack of thunder split the air. A torrent of rain came out of nowhere, and lightning flashed all around him. Andy heard a chorus of deep unearthly voices crying out in alarm, and he felt the earth beneath him start to shake and pull apart. It looked to Andy like the entire world was about to come to an end.

"*Aaah!* Somebody help me!" he screamed.

Then, just as he was about to be swallowed up by a particularly large crack in the ground that was spreading toward his feet, everything stopped. The rain disappeared, the thunder ceased, and the supernaturally loud voices were silenced.

A soft, almost amused voice came from the hut. "Hoku! You silly bird. Why didn't you tell me you were bringing a guest? I would have turned off the security system."

Security system? Andy wondered.

Andy stepped away from the long crack of earth his feet were straddling. Turning around, he saw a kind-looking elderly woman standing in the doorway of the hut. She was wearing a blue muumuu and had a lei of pink hibiscus blossoms around her neck.

The woman smiled. It was such a bright, beautiful smile that Andy couldn't help smiling back.

"I hope you weren't hurt," the woman said. She motioned for Andy to come closer.

Andy hesitated, glancing at the tikis lying facedown in the tall grass.

"Oh, don't worry about them," she said, chuckling. "They won't bother you now."

Andy walked carefully toward the old woman, stepping gingerly around the fallen statues. "Are you sure you can control them?" he asked. "They seemed awfully angry."

"Of course I can," the old woman replied. "They are meant to keep out those who aren't wanted, and you are welcome here. You didn't think . . ." She turned and gave Hoku a stern glance. The bird fluttered to her shoulder, looking embarrassed.

"Hoku! What did you tell him?" the woman said sharply.

Hoku hid her head beneath her wing. The old woman shook a gnarled finger at the bird. "I've warned you about this kind of mischief before. If you don't stop with your tricks, I'll have you put back on your perch for good, do you understand me?"

Hoku nodded, her head still firmly beneath her wing.

"You knew?" Andy shouted. "I trusted you, you dumb bird! And I nearly died for it!"

Andy was angry that she'd tricked him into thinking he was being attacked by supernatural deities. There was no doubt the danger had been real, but it would have caused Andy a lot less anxiety if he'd known that the tikis were just part of an elaborate security system.

Hoku shot Andy a sheepish look and said, "Hoku is sorry, sorry she is. Just having fun, fun with Andy."

Fun? Andy had some strong words to share with Hoku about her idea of fun, but he decided to let the issue rest. He sighed, letting his irritation fade, and said, "Don't worry about it. Just tell me next time."

Hoku removed her head from under her wing and hopped happily on the woman's shoulder, apparently glad that all was forgiven.

The old woman motioned for Andy to enter the hut, and Andy stepped up the wooden stairway toward the bamboo door. As he drew close, the woman held out her hand.

"I'm Madame Wiki," she said. "You are welcome here."

Andy shook her hand. "Andy Stanley," he said.

Madame Wiki's eyes widened with surprise. "Ned's grandson? Albert didn't tell me who you were when he found you. He only said that he'd rescued you at sea. I had to perform one of my most powerful spells to drive the chill from your bones."

"Spells?" Andy asked, confused.

Madame Wiki gave him a shrewd look. "You sound surprised. Don't you believe in magic?"

Andy shifted his feet uncomfortably. "I've always assumed magic is no more than superstition."

The old woman laughed. "Superstition has nothing to do with it!" Her eyes twinkled as she looked deep into Andy's. "These islands are filled with magic. Come inside the Enchanted Tiki Room and see for yourself."

Chapter Fourteen
The Enchanted Tiki Room

The first thing Andy noticed when he walked inside the hut was how dimly lit it was.

Unable to see much of anything, Andy was forced to rely on his other senses. He smelled a faint whiff of coconut, pineapple, wet bamboo, and fragrant tropical flowers.

He allowed Madame Wiki's hand on his arm to

guide him along, and soon his eyes adjusted to the dim light. In the center of the room was a large fountain surrounded by orchids. Madame Wiki ushered Andy to a chair nearby.

Andy took his seat and watched as Madame Wiki began waving a bamboo stick in an intricate pattern and murmuring some words in what he could only assume was Hawaiian.

What is she doing? Andy wondered. A moment later he realized what it was. *Oh, I see. She's reciting some kind of magic spell. Doesn't she know there's no such thing as—*

Andy didn't have time to finish the thought. A steady glow began to emanate from inside the fountain. Soon the orchids that surrounded the base reacted as well, blooming. There was an explosion of color like nothing Andy had ever seen before as the delicate flowers opened. Even in the dimness of the room, Andy could see that the reds, purples, and pinks were absolutely stunning.

Then, to Andy's amazement, the flowers began to sing in lovely high voices.

I can't believe it! How is this possible?

Hoku flapped up to a perch near the ceiling of the hut and chirped happily.

Andy listened to the beautiful chorus. Noticing his slack jaw and wide, uncomprehending gaze, Madame Wiki chuckled and said, "The islands are filled with surprises. The menehune, our magical little people, ensure that their mysteries are kept safe." She gestured around the hut. "They blessed this place and made it a sanctuary for the rarest of our magical flowers and the most intelligent of birds in all Polynesia. The Akamai are a species of mystical birds that are capable not only of speech, but of reasoning as well . . . like Hoku."

"Amazing," Andy whispered softly, still entranced by the beautiful music.

Madame Wiki nodded. "And that's why four of your grandfather's friends—Sherman, Burns, Bruns, and Boag— were enlisted to design the security system, to keep out anyone who would threaten their existence. Each of the flowers and birds in the Tiki Room is priceless. There are many poachers who would love to steal them."

Andy thought about the tikis and how convinced he had been that they were real. As he stared at the singing flowers and up at Hoku, he realized that the tikis could hardly compare to real magic.

"The flowers' song is said to soothe the soul and inspire courage in all who hear it. Many ancient warriors swore by their powers and would listen to them before going to battle," Madame Wiki said.

She's right, Andy thought. *It feels like the song is moving through my entire body. It's so strange!*

Suddenly, he remembered why he was there. He felt awkward interrupting the singing flowers and waited until the last notes of their chorus died away before turning to Madame Wiki.

"Madame Wiki, my grandfather sent me here to search for something called the Tiki Key. He said it was very important that I find it and use it to retrieve the

Pailina Pendant. Do you know anything about these items?"

Madame Wiki was quiet for a long moment, and Andy began to wonder whether she'd heard him. "Did your grandfather tell you how dangerous it would be for you to do this?" she finally replied.

Andy gulped. "Well, kind of," he admitted. "My grandfather told me that finding the key would be dangerous. He seemed to think that the danger would make the adventure more fun, if you can believe that."

Madame Wiki laughed. "That sounds like Ned."

Andy gave her a serious look. "Can you help me find it? I know that my chances of success are probably low, but I'm willing to do everything I can to stop this Phink person from getting his hands on it first."

Madame Wiki nodded. "I can and will." Then, to Andy's surprise, she clapped her hands loudly. "José, Fritz, Pierre, Michael!" she called. "I require your assistance."

Andy looked around, confused. Who was she talking to? By the sound of their names, he assumed that several burly soldiers might appear to protect him as he moved to the next stage of his quest.

He wasn't at all prepared for the four beautiful parrots that flew down from somewhere near the ceiling to perches positioned above the magical fountain. Each landed next to a hanging seashell that had its name printed on it. A warm glow suffused the dark hut as the birds alighted on their perches, and Andy gazed around in appreciation at the beautiful setting.

"Amazing," he repeated, taking in the carvings on the wall. The pillars holding up the hut were carved as well, with angry-looking faces etched into them. *It's like looking at an illustration in a fairy tale book.*

"Bonjour, Madame Wiki! I see that we have a guest, no?" Pierre, the first bird to have landed on his perch, said with a suave French accent.

"Top o' the mornin' to ya, laddie!" Michael called with a lilting Irish accent. The other two birds, Fritz and José, chimed in as well, offering their greetings.

"Hello," said Andy. He grinned, feeling a renewed

wonder at hearing the birds talk. Like Hoku, each of the parrots seemed very smart and able to communicate with humans.

Andy noticed that each bird's plumage was different colors. Pierre's feathers were red, white, and blue, while Michael's colors were green, white, and orange. Being an extremely sharp-witted boy, Andy quickly realized that each had the colors of the flag of his native country.

Fritz spoke next, in a thick German accent: "Frau Wiki, vat did you call us for? I vas in deep debate with José about the reason humans sometimes refer to other humans as 'birdbrains.'"

"*Sí*," José added. "I was telling *mi amigo* here that the term is a high compliment on a person's intelligence. After all, nobody is smarter than a bird!"

"*Nein!*" Fritz said. "You are wrong, my South American friend. It is an insult!"

Andy stifled a chuckle. He didn't want to offend José by telling him that Fritz was right.

Madame Wiki paid no attention to the argument the birds were having. Instead, she clapped her hands, silencing them.

"Gentlemen, the time has come. Andy Stanley has been sent by Ned Lostmore to retrieve the item that we've been protecting," she said sternly.

"Saints preserve us!" Michael exclaimed. "You don't mean . . ."

Madame Wiki nodded. "I do."

"*Ach du lieber!*" Fritz cried. "Using the key is dangerous! Are you sure? If this boy tries to unlock the door, he could be kaput!"

Madame Wiki, noting Andy's paleness, put a comforting hand on his shoulder. "Don't worry, boy. Ned wouldn't have sent you if he didn't think you could do it."

Andy wasn't so sure. What did his grandfather *really* know about him at all?

Madame Wiki turned her eyes to the ceiling and let out a long, low whistle. Then she lifted her hands above her head. "It is time, my friends."

Chapter Fifteen
The Tiki Key

At the sound of Madame Wiki's voice, there was a sudden rush of wings, and dozens of hanging perches covered with flowers descended majestically from the ceiling. Seated on them were hundreds of beautiful Akamai.

Madame Wiki waved her hands and murmured what Andy assumed was an ancient Polynesian spell. The soft voices of the flowers filled the room again. The birds, taking their cue from the flowers, joined in. Then, to Andy's surprise, the carved pillars that held up the hut began to chant.

Andy wheeled around and saw that the carvings on the walls had taken up a rhythmic percussion beat. Their arms pumped up and down, banging on loud Hawaiian drums.

Andy felt the hair on the back of his neck stand on end. His heart thumped wildly. *How can this be happening? It feels like a dream, but I know I'm awake.*

He looked at Madame Wiki. Her eyes were closed. Behind her, the fountain glowed with magical energy. A narrow stream of water rose from its center. Madame Wiki began to sway back and forth as she whispered the words of the spell.

Andy gasped as the beam of water rose over ten feet in the air. *How can it do that? It shouldn't even be possible!*

The music grew in intensity, the chant coming from the pillars getting louder and louder. The voices of the birds resonated in a warbling chorus, high and sweet.

Madame Wiki continued swaying back and forth, lost in a trance.

Andy felt a fluttering in the pit of his stomach, and his palms began to sweat. Dizziness overwhelmed him. Andy gripped his stomach with both hands as nausea washed over him.

The strange feeling of otherworldly energy was becoming too much. He thought he might faint if it went on too long.

Just when he felt sure he couldn't take another minute, the hut was plunged into darkness. A flash of lightning shone through the shutters, quickly followed by a splitting crack of thunder that echoed outside the Tiki Room.

And then, as suddenly as it had started, the music stopped. The gentle mystical light the fountain provided returned.

Andy relished the newly restored quiet and tried to calm his nerves. *Thank goodness that's over. I don't think I could have taken much more of it!*

Looking up, he saw that the birds were gone. Only Hoku remained, sitting on Madame Wiki's shoulder and crooning softly.

Andy looked down at his shaking hands and was startled to find something in his lap that hadn't been there before.

It was a wooden box, its lid open. On a bed of woven palm fronds in the box rested a small item. It had a long shaft made from polished koa wood. Carved into the top of it was a frowning face.

Andy knew at once that it was what he'd come looking for.

"The Tiki Key."

Chapter Sixteen
Escape?

Andy stared at the key. He had so many questions: Where had the birds gone? How had the water in the fountain mystically risen into the air? How had the carved pillars been able to come to life? And most important, where had the key come from?

But before he could ask a single question, a noise outside interrupted his thoughts.

Madame Wiki moved close and lowered her head

next to his ear. "The traps around the hut are still down," she whispered. "We have intruders."

Andy felt the blood rush from his face. "What do we do?" he whispered back. He could hear the rustling of people moving outside and had the feeling that the door to the hut might burst open at any moment.

Putting a finger to her lips, Madame Wiki motioned for Andy to follow her. The two crossed the room and came to a stop in front of one of the pillars that had just moments before been alive. Madame Wiki pressed a small carving on the pillar, and the base swung open, revealing a tiny lever. She pulled it and a small door at the back of the hut appeared, a tunnel beyond it disappearing into darkness.

"Go!" she said. "At the end of the tunnel is a small boat. Tell the owner that Madame Wiki has need of his help. He will take you to Nanea, the mother of all volcanoes. There you'll find what you seek."

"Wait," Andy replied. He glanced nervously behind Madame Wiki. The footfalls were growing louder, and

Andy could have sworn he heard the sound of weapons being drawn. "What's going to happen to you?"

Madame Wiki looked deep into his eyes. "I'll be fine. Stay strong, my boy!"

Andy felt Madame Wiki's powerful hands gently turn him around and give him a small push toward the tunnel. He didn't like the idea of leaving her behind.

I can't just run away. What would Grandfather think of me fleeing like a coward? If I really do have the Lostmore Spirit, now's the time to prove it.

Andy turned away from the escape route and pulled his fountain pen from his pocket. Remembering what Ned had told him, he prepared to activate the atomic pulse emitter.

Madame Wiki looked at him, a confused expression on her face.

"What is—"

She was interrupted by the crash of the Enchanted Tiki Room's door blasting open. Standing in the doorway was a group of fierce-looking men. They wore dark clothing and bared their teeth in fearsome grins. Andy saw that they carried knives and large pouches.

Poachers! he thought. *They've come for the birds!*

Andy didn't waste a second. He aimed the pen toward the would-be thieves and pressed down on the cap.

A tremendous boom rocked the hut. The poachers nearest the doorway were caught by surprise and flew backward.

Madame Wiki was impressed. "That's quite a pen!" she exclaimed.

Andy grinned and turned toward Madame Wiki. But there was no time to gloat. The blast had not knocked out all his foes, and a large pair of hands suddenly gripped him from behind. A second pair ripped the Tiki Key from his fingers.

"Andy Stanley. I've heard so much about you," someone called from the shadows in a refined female voice.

Andy had just enough time to see a girl a few years older than him, clothed completely in black, step in front of him before a rough cloth bag was pulled over his head. This time he recognized the face at once. It was Abigail Awol!

Andy struggled heroically, but it was useless. *I've lost the key! My very first assignment for my grandfather and I've failed. What kind of Keymaster can't hold on to a key?*

He felt a deep pang of disappointment. But he didn't have time to dwell on his failure, for mere seconds later his vision began to blur and the world around him faded to black.

Chapter Seventeen
The Poachers

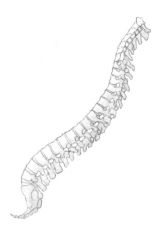

The first thing Andy noticed when he regained consciousness was the ringing in his ears. His head felt like it was filled with cotton, and he had a horrible taste in his mouth. His eyelids felt like they each weighed fifty pounds. When he forced them open, he saw several faces leaning over him.

Poachers!

Andy was suddenly wide awake! In spite of his

aching body, he scooted backward, banging his head into a metal bar.

Andy looked around. He was on a bed! What he'd hit his head on was no more than an iron headboard.

Where am I?

Andy scrambled upright, searching his pocket for the Zoomwriter. How was he going to defend himself without it? But it was no use. The pen was gone.

"Hold on there, sonny. No reason to raise an alarm!" one of his captors said. The man glanced at the other three men. "At ease, boys. You're scaring the lad."

Andy stared at the poacher who had spoken. Everything about his appearance was primal—ferocious. He wore an eye patch and had a gruesome scar down one side of his face. And yet, he spoke with an elegant English accent. He seemed to be the one in charge.

The man offered Andy his hand. "Nice to meet you. I'm Samuel Sanders."

Andy shook the man's hand. "Andy Stanley," he said, confused. *Why is he being so ... polite?*

Sanders smiled and gestured to his companions.

"This is Jack Simms, Phineas Crumpt, and Bill Nickels," he said.

The others responded with quick nods.

Sanders turned back to Andy. "And we already know who you are. We work for your grandfather."

Andy must have still been disoriented from the chemicals they had used to knock him out. His head was swimming, and he was having a hard time processing what he was hearing. "What's that you just said?" he asked.

Sanders chuckled. "We work for Ned and the Jungle Explorers' Society. You've been brought to Base Camp Alpha. Bit of a surprise, eh? Sorry 'bout the bag on your head. Not the best way to introduce ourselves, but I assure you it was necessary. Your grandfather's plans have to be followed to a tee, but they always work."

Andy knew his grandfather was a strange man, but had he really told these men to kidnap him? *How do I know I can trust them? What if they really work for Phink? What if this is a trap?*

Sanders didn't seem to notice Andy's hesitation. "Put on your shoes and come with us," he ordered. "That incredible pen of yours is on the nightstand, by the way. I don't know what it is, exactly, but it knocked out three of our best operatives. Your granddad sure knows his gadgets."

Andy picked up the pen and tentatively followed the men. He had no way of knowing if they really were who they claimed to be, but they *had* given back the Zoomwriter. Besides, Andy reasoned, it was either follow them outside or stay in the dimly lit hut.

The group emerged in what looked like a tribal village. Upon closer inspection, however, Andy saw that the huts were actually constructed with high-quality building materials made to look like bamboo. Glancing through one of the windows, he realized that the disguise was intended to conceal the modern interiors of the buildings, which seemed to house the Society's ultra-secret communications equipment.

Amazing! They're hiding in plain sight!

Andy followed the men into a large hut in the center of the village.

So this is what a base of operations for the Society looks like, Andy thought. He gazed around, trying to process what he was seeing.

The room was filled from floor to ceiling with high-tech surveillance equipment. The whine of radio static and blips of the radar screens mingled with the hubbub of low conversation, typewriter keys, and Morse code transmissions. It looked like pictures of military outposts he'd seen in magazines.

The familiar aroma of fresh coffee, incongruous in such a remote jungle setting, filled the quarters. It reminded Andy that he hadn't eaten in a while, and his stomach growled in response.

Gazing around the room, Andy noticed several operatives poised at different stations. He studied their faces. Something about them was familiar. Then it hit him. *They're the people from the funeral!*

Rusty Bucketts, the man with the steel ball for an

eye, stood over a radio. Next to him, holding two clip-boards, were the belly-dancing conjoined twins, Betty and Dotty. Next to the sisters was Molly the mime, and standing regally at a radar station was Cedric, the witch doctor, still in his mask, but now wearing a safari suit in place of his robes.

Sanders called the group to attention. As one, they looked up and burst into loud cheers!

What's all this? Andy thought. *Who are they cheering for?*

Andy looked behind him to see if someone else had entered the hut, but there was no one there. Were they cheering for *him*?

Rusty rushed forward and pumped Andy's hand up and down. He grinned widely, making his handlebar mustache reach high up on his ruddy cheeks.

"Well done, Master Andy. Well done indeed! You've followed the plan perfectly! Your grandfather must be so proud."

Andy smiled back, confused. "I . . . I don't understand,"

he faltered. But before he could continue, the twins had wrapped him up in a four-armed hug. "We knew you could do it!" they said in unison. And then, to Andy's surprise, they kissed both of his cheeks at the same time, one on either side.

Molly the mime cheered the loudest of all, repeatedly thumping him on the back and going on about his bravery.

She really is a terrible mime, Andy thought.

He blushed furiously. *They must be confused about what actually happened at the Enchanted Tiki Room. They think I saved the Tiki Key. They don't know that I lost the key to Abigail Awol.*

With a sinking feeling, Andy realized he had to tell them the truth.

He held up his hands for silence. The applause died down, and everyone looked at him expectantly.

"I'm really sorry to disappoint you," Andy said awkwardly. "I don't deserve your praise. The truth is, Abigail Awol stole the Tiki Key from me. I couldn't stop it from happening."

Andy stared at the ground, shamefaced. But the moment was quickly interrupted by Sanders, who placed his hand on Andy's shoulder. "But that's exactly what was supposed to happen, lad!"

Andy looked up at Sanders, completely lost. "It was?"

Sanders grinned. "Of course!" He reached into the pouch on his belt and withdrew an exact replica of the Tiki Key. Andy stared at it, dumbfounded.

"There's another one?" Andy asked.

"This is the real Tiki Key," Sanders explained. "The one Abigail stole is a fake. It's equipped with a tracking device that will allow us to follow Professor Phink." He flashed Andy a conspiratorial smirk and gestured around the room at the various surveillance stations.

"We've known the location of the Tiki Key for years. Well, how could we not? Ned was the one who hid it. What we don't know is the location of the locked chamber that holds the Pailina Pendant."

"Grandfather mentioned the pendant," Andy said.

"He said we must keep it out of Phink's hands, but he didn't say why. What is it?"

Rusty cleared his throat. "The Pailina Pendant is a legendary artifact. It is said to keep an evil Hawaiian god named Kapu prisoner. Kapu was imprisoned by his brother, Kane, over a thousand years ago. If the legends are true, he is a monster, capable of terrible destruction."

Andy's pulse quickened. He'd seen real magic and had little doubt that what he was being told was actually possible. *A real Hawaiian god?* he thought. *Like a living version of the statues protecting the Tiki Room?* Andy shuddered at the memory of the tikis he'd knocked over. Those had terrified him, and they hadn't even been real. How horrible would an actual god be? Especially after having been imprisoned for a thousand years!

"The pendant can only be removed with a special key called the Kapu Key," Rusty continued. "We tried for years to find that key, but Phink got to it first. Then, a few weeks ago, we received intelligence that Phink had found the entrance to Kapu's hiding place. But knowing where the entrance is isn't enough. The doorway is magically protected. It can only be opened with the Tiki Key. We knew Phink would be searching for the key so that he could get inside, so we came up with a plan to lure him to the Tiki Room. If he thought he had the key, we knew we could follow him to the entrance. It's the only way to get our hands on the key that unlocks the pendant."

Andy felt a surge of anger. "Wait a minute. So what you're saying is that my grandfather arranged for me to be the bait? All of this was just so that Professor Phink would follow me to the Tiki Room and steal the fake key from me?"

The entire group nodded enthusiastically.

"It's a race to get to the pendant before Phink can take it and loose the evil god upon the world," Rusty said. "And you've helped us gain an advantage. Now that Phink knows the location of the pendant, the Society must take that dangerous artifact under our protection."

The others in the group nodded.

"But won't the Pailina Pendant be safe if Phink isn't able to open the door to the chamber? We could just hang on to the real key and not let him get inside," Andy said.

The others exchanged worried glances. "We thought about that already," said Rusty. "But we can't take a chance that Phink won't find some other way in."

"The ancient Hawaiians did what they could to protect the pendant," chimed in Betty. "But with modern explosives and machinery, there's no guarantee their spells will hold. And there's no telling to what lengths the professor will go to get inside once he learns that his Tiki Key is a fake."

Dotty nodded agreement with her sister and added, "That's why time is of the essence. Phink will try the Tiki Key first. But he won't wait long to try something else. Once we know where the door is, we have to move fast. It's imperative that we get our hands on the Kapu Key before he can make other plans to get inside."

Andy nodded. He understood the gravity of the situation, but he couldn't help feeling betrayed. He'd believed that he and Madame Wiki were in terrible danger, and the entire time it had just been one big joke?

"Why didn't you just tell me what you had planned?" he asked, trying to hold in his fury. "Why did you have to lie and manipulate me? And why should I believe anything you say now, if everything that has happened so far has all been one big lie?"

Why couldn't Ned have told him what was going on? He had said Andy was the only one he could trust, but it seemed he had trusted everyone *but* Andy.

From the back of the room, Albert appeared with Hoku on his shoulder. Like the others, he was smiling at Andy.

"I'm sorry to have kept you in the dark, son," Albert said. "But we were under strict orders from your grandfather not to tell you anything. He knew the only way for you to find your courage was to truly believe that the fate of the world rested on your shoulders. And in a way, it did. We needed you to make sure the fake key landed in Phink's possession. Abigail is perceptive. She would have seen through you had you known it was all an act."

Albert tousled Andy's hair. "When you stood up to Sanders and his 'poachers' instead of taking the escape route, you nearly threw the whole plan into jeopardy. We assumed you would run out the back of the Tiki Room to safety. We were planning to do our fake ambush there. We've spent a long time infiltrating Phink's organization so that Abigail would believe we were on her side. We knew once she had the key, the rest of the details wouldn't matter to her, but we had to make it look real."

"But you stood by my side even when you were afraid," a voice said. Andy turned and saw Madame Wiki. The medicine woman gave him a gentle smile. "I don't know many boys your age who would have acted so bravely."

Andy blushed a deep shade of crimson. *Brave? Me?*

The praise from Madame Wiki helped ease his feelings of betrayal somewhat.

"You have been invaluable to the mission, and we don't want you to think that your actions have gone unappreciated," Albert said. "In fact, as a token of our gratitude . . ."

Andy watched as Albert removed a small medal from his pocket. He handed it to Madame Wiki, who pinned it to Andy's shirt, right over his chest pocket.

Albert gestured to the medal pinned on Andy's chest. "Andy Stanley, for showing such backbone in the face of extreme danger—perceived or otherwise—we award you the Silver Sacroiliac."

Andy looked at the medal. It resembled a strange series of bones. It was, in fact, the shape of a backbone, with every vertebra represented in perfect detail.

Albert cleared his throat and held up both hands above his head. "Ladies and gentlemen, members of the Jungle Explorers' Society, it is my pleasure to announce that phase one of our plan to retrieve the Pailina Pendant is complete thanks to Andy Stanley, the grandson of our fearless leader, Ned Lostmore."

Everyone in the room clapped.

I guess I really did help! Andy thought. *Maybe if I can keep proving myself, the Society will actually make me a member!*

The mere thought of it gave him a thrill. Andy's mind raced, trying unsuccessfully to formulate a response. "Thank you . . . I . . . I don't know what to say," he said finally.

And he really didn't.

Sanders relieved him of his awkwardness. "Thank you is more than good enough! We expect great things from you, my lad!"

Sanders handed Andy the real Tiki Key. It was noticeably heavier than the fake one.

"As our Keymaster, this is yours to protect. Guard it well, son."

Andy nodded and beamed at his new friends. Never in a million years would he have expected to feel proud at being part of a group with the strange people he'd seen at his grandfather's "funeral." Never. But things had changed, and Andy was surprised to find that he felt quite good about his current company.

"Now I don't know about the rest of you, but I'm starving," Sanders continued in a loud, happy shout. "And I would guess that a boy of Andy's age is twice as hungry as I am. So, without further ado, let the feast begin!"

Andy watched in awe as people began setting up tables and bringing in huge trays of delicious-looking food from a room hidden somewhere in the back of the hut.

For the first time since his adventure had begun, Andy felt extraordinarily content. In spite of all the danger he'd experienced so far, he knew he would go through it all again just to be there at that very moment.

I'm actually having dinner with the Jungle Explorers' Society! he thought. And then, gazing around at all the happy faces and the generous feast, he whispered quietly under his breath, "I wish this night would go on forever."

Chapter Eighteen
Phase Two

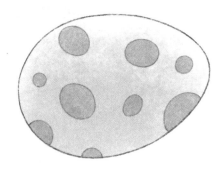

The next morning, Andy found himself aboard Albert Awol's boat, surrounded by the uniquely gifted members of the Jungle Explorers' Society.

"We should arrive near the base of the Nanea volcano in about ten minutes," Albert said. "Let's go over the plan one more time."

Andy glanced at the scruffy sea captain and

suppressed an inward groan. *We've already been over this a dozen times.*

Rusty spoke first. "Aye, aye, cap'n!" he said, offering Albert a crisp salute. He turned to address the group assembled in the boat.

"All right, you all remember the drill. Betty and Dotty?"

The twins, who had been whispering quietly to each other, suddenly sat up straight. "We'll cover the entrance and signal when we have the all clear," they recited in unison.

"And we've got our usual defenses should there be any trouble," added Betty, the twin on the left.

Andy watched as the women reached into the silk sashes in their belly-dancing costumes and removed handfuls of sharply pointed metal stars. Andy recognized them as *shuriken*, deadly throwing stars often used by assassins.

"I'll be guarding the left flank," said Cedric, who was wearing a set of elegant jade robes and his tribal mask.

"Of course, I've come prepared with *my* usual choice of weapon as well."

Andy had assumed that because Cedric wore a traditional mask, he would be carrying a spear or some other old-fashioned weapon. Instead, the doctor held up a small object that looked to Andy like a festive blue robin's egg covered with purple polka dots.

"Righto, Cedric!" Rusty shouted happily.

The other members of the Society seemed to know what the object was, and the entire group burst into a fit of nervous laughter. Albert leaned away from the captain's wheel so that Andy could hear him above the roar of the boat engines and let Andy in on the joke.

"Cedric is not only a gifted witch doctor, but also an explosives expert. He was decorated by the king for his bravery during the Great War."

Albert nodded toward the small egg. "Quite the amateur artist, too. He can't help decorating his bombs with a little . . . creative flair."

Cedric put the egg-shaped bomb in his robe pocket and nodded to Molly the mime.

Andy saw that Molly had applied a fresh coat of white face paint and a jaunty black beret for the occasion.

He studied her skeptically. He felt fairly confident that the others knew what they were doing, but he wasn't so sure about her. After all, who could possibly be afraid of a mime? *Still, she is a member of the Jungle Explorers' Society. They must see something in her,* he mused.

"Okay, I'm prepared for this. I practiced all last night and I can say without a doubt that I am ready for this. Totally ready. Can't wait. Did I say I was ready? I'm ready . . ." Molly chattered.

Andy tried not to laugh when she produced a set of juggling balls and began tossing them into the air. The others on the boat nodded appreciatively, never cracking a smile.

As Andy shook his head in bewilderment at the others' reaction to Molly, Hoku flew down from Albert's shoulder and landed on Andy's knee.

"What's your job, Andy? What's Andy Stanley's job?" she squawked.

All eyes turned to look at him.

Andy recited the mission briefing he'd been given after the feast the previous night.

"My job is to signal the group when Phink reveals the location of the door. I'm to avoid Phink's soldiers and keep my pen at the ready." For emphasis, he removed his pen from his pocket.

Everyone, including Hoku, nodded. Andy grinned and replaced the weapon in his pocket. His part seemed easy enough, but what if Phink saw him? What then?

The thought made him shudder. He'd heard so much about the ruthless villain. He wasn't sure he was prepared to face him one-on-one.

Stay calm, he reminded himself. *You can do this. It's your job to watch for Phink, not confront him. Simple.*

Albert spoke up. "Remember, we don't know anything about where the pendant is actually kept. But if Madame Wiki is right about the legend—"

Andy perked up. "Wait, what legend?" he asked. "No one mentioned a legend."

Andy watched as the others in the group exchanged nervous glances. *Not again. What aren't they telling me this time?* He hated being the last one to know important information.

"Will someone please tell me what's going on?" he begged. "It seems like ever since I started on this adventure, people have been keeping secrets from me. I nearly died to get you this far. I think I've earned the truth."

Andy sat up straighter, looking from one face to the next. It felt good to stand up for himself for once.

An awkward silence fell over the group. No one seemed willing to speak. After a few moments, Rusty piped up.

"Kapu is said to wear the pendant around his neck. Legend has it that the holder of the pendant can control Kapu, but removing it will awaken the god, who is sure to be hungry after such a long sleep. And, well . . ."

"Well, what?" Andy asked.

"He eats humans," Rusty finished. Then he gave Andy a level stare. "This mission cannot fail. Getting our hands on both the Kapu Key and the Tiki Key is the only way to make sure they're kept safe. Phink is part of a dark organization that will stop at nothing to gain power. If they have an evil god on their side willing to obey their every order, the world is doomed."

Andy thought he had understood the full importance of the mission before, but this new information weighed heavily on him. Trying to get those keys under his protection was likely to be difficult and violent. Phink didn't sound like the type of person to go down without a fight.

Why me, Grandfather? Andy wondered. *Did you really believe that I could do this?* He tried to gather his courage, but he felt shaky and nervous. The bravado he'd shown before had faded away as the true purpose of their mission had come to light. *I'm only a kid. Can I really be the Keymaster?*

Rusty interrupted his anxious thoughts.

"No matter what happens when we confront Phink—if something, somehow, goes wrong and the fight takes us to the inside of the volcano—make sure you stay clear of Kapu. Understood? And whatever happens, don't let Phink use that key."

"What if Phink tries to take the key by force . . . if he uses a g-gun or something?" Andy stuttered.

Rusty laid a meaty hand on his shoulder. "You're the Keymaster. We'll do our best to protect you. But keep that pen of yours at the ready. You might need it."

Andy gulped and nodded. He fingered the real Tiki Key on the ring at his belt. As Keymaster, he was supposed to protect it with his life, though he hoped it wouldn't come to that.

The mood had grown somber. Nobody spoke for the next few minutes as Albert's boat approached a hidden cove. Behind the trees, towering over them, was the gigantic volcano Nanea.

Maybe the legend isn't true, Andy thought. *What if*

Phink is just crazy, and there is no evil god imprisoned inside a volcano? After all, the whole thing does sound pretty far-fetched.

Andy didn't want to believe a word of the legend. Everything in him that trusted in science and logic balked at the idea of superstition. But ever since he'd met his grandfather and seen Madame Wiki's magic, his mind had been in a state of confused panic. It was like finding out that all the fears of his childhood—like the monster under the bed and the bogeyman—were real, not just stories told to frighten young children.

The boat pulled up to the shore, and Albert used the bowline to tie it fast to a fallen tree trunk. Andy felt a surge of anxiety. Only one thought kept repeating itself over and over in his mind, and it was the only one that mattered. It was the only way he would ever get safely home again.

The only way out is to go forward, Andy thought.

Gathering what little courage he had, Andy stepped from the boat.

Chapter Nineteen
The Volcano Gate

The group silently climbed the slope that led to the base of Nanea, careful not to call attention to themselves. The Hodges Zoomwriter sat safely in Andy's pocket. He wanted to hold it—to draw comfort from knowing the device was ready to protect him—but he feared that he would grip it too tightly and snap the barrel in two.

Maybe Phink won't be there, he thought. *And then*

we can just forget this whole thing. We can all go back to the base and have a good laugh.

But even as he told himself these things, there was a part of him that knew it wouldn't be the case. All the way up the tree-laden slope, Andy kept telling himself to calm down, to push aside the anxiety he was feeling. The truth was, he didn't know what would be waiting for him when they got to the top of the hill. Would Professor Phink and Abigail be there? Would there be an army of henchmen? What if Phink had enlisted the help of the witch doctor who had shrunk his grandfather's head? Worse still, what if Andy ended up the same way? Just about anything would be better than that. The thought of being shipped home to his horrified parents as a talking shrunken head like Ned was almost more than he could bear.

Andy tried his best to quell such thoughts. *Be brave! Stay calm. You can do this! That's not going to happen to you.*

But the thoughts still kept coming. By the time he'd

actually crested the hill that looked down into the valley by the volcano's base, he'd worked himself up into such a state of anxiety that he thought he would pass out.

Andy looked over the ridge. There was nothing to be seen. The long, well-maintained path that led to the base of the mountain was empty except for a few tropical birds in a nearby tree.

Andy wiped a shaking palm across his sweaty forehead. *Professor Phink isn't here!*

Perhaps all the fancy surveillance equipment the Society had used to track the fake Tiki Key was malfunctioning.

A new hope flared in Andy's chest as he thought about another possibility. Maybe the professor had already been there and had been unable to find the secret gate that led inside. Maybe he'd just gone home. . . .

CRACK! From out of nowhere came a sizzling blast of white heat. Andy stared at an area just above his head where a palm tree had been neatly cut in half, its trunk still smoking.

What in the world?

"Get down!" Rusty shouted.

Andy felt the man's big hand push him roughly to the earth as another sizzling blast fried a grove of papaya trees. The entire group had fallen flat on the ground, hoping not to be seen by whatever was firing in their direction.

The twins were the first to spot the source of the attack. Behind them, through the trees on the left, was a gathering of people dressed all in black. In the center of the group, Andy saw a tall man wearing a waistcoat and top hat. He assumed this was Phink. The villain was shouting orders to a girl seated behind a huge cannon-like weapon that looked to Andy like something straight out of a Jules Verne novel.

Another thunderous blast shook the earth. Andy covered his head with his hands, protecting himself against the heat. He heard a loud *BOOM!* as the fiery charge struck the side of the volcano.

Suddenly, Andy understood what was happening.

They weren't being shot at. Professor Phink was blasting the wall of the volcano, trying to create an opening!

Albert spoke in a low voice. "I bet he doesn't know where the door is. Maybe our intelligence was wrong—"

Cedric interrupted him, saying, "Sorry to disappoint you, old sport, but I believe he knows exactly what he's doing." He gestured to the spot on the side of the mountain where the blast had recently hit. "The reason we couldn't locate the door was because it was covered up. The last time the volcano erupted, the lava must have hardened over the entrance. Why didn't we think of that before?"

"What do we do?" Andy asked. "With that laser cannon thing he's got down there, he could fry us all like bacon."

"I say we wait," Albert answered.

Hoku nodded enthusiastically in agreement. "Wait. Yes, wait. Hoku likes to wait. Especially back in the Tiki Room. Wait, wait. Go back and wait."

Albert rolled his eyes at the terrified bird. "Hoku! We're not leaving until this is done."

Hoku lowered her head and fluffed out her feathers, muttering darkly. It was obvious to Andy that she was as scared as he was.

A sudden movement out of the corner of his eye caused him to jump.

The next thing he knew, the twins were on their feet, shouting. Throwing stars flew from their fingers like bullets from a gun, eliciting shouts of alarm and grunts of painful surprise from a group of black-clad figures that had been sneaking up on them. The dense jungle had provided Phink's henchmen with plenty of cover, and if not for the twins' quick reflexes, the whole group would have been captured—or killed!

The fight that followed was spectacular. Andy was shocked to see just how well trained the Jungle Explorers' Society actually was.

Rusty popped his steel eyeball from its socket and, drawing a slingshot from his belt, pelted one of the biggest attackers in the forehead, felling him in one shot.

"Take that!" he shouted as he charged at the attackers.

"For the Society!" he yelled.

Andy saw the effect it had on Phink's men. One of them didn't want anything to do with the burly explorer and immediately turned tail and ran. But the others must have been made of sterner stuff. The soldiers met Rusty head-on. Soon there was a wild, snarling fight with fists flying everywhere and knives slashing through the air. Rusty fought like an enraged tiger, and where his fists landed, teeth and jaws were broken.

Dotty and Betty were just as effective. The twins worked in perfect harmony, whipping throwing stars at their enemies and sending them screaming to the ground.

Andy heard the sisters' voices above the din, one of them singing a battle song in a low alto and the other a soprano. The harmonic effect sounded a lot like a bagpipe, and it had an eerie quality that made the little hairs on Andy's arms stand on end.

When the twins had used up their store of throwing stars, they twirled and leapt into the air, using their conjoined hips to their advantage. Their acrobatics not only put distance between them and the stunned soldiers, but also gave them a surprising edge. Andy watched, amazed, as two pairs of spinning back kicks hit three of the attackers, knocking them out cold.

Cedric stood, egg-shaped bomb at the ready, waiting for the right moment. Spotting another group of Phink's attackers heading up the hill, he shouted an incomprehensible battle cry and flung the egg as hard as he could manage in their direction. The colorful bomb exploded on impact, taking out nearly half of the hill along with Phink's men.

Hoku flapped and scratched with her talons at a thin attacker with an ugly scar running down his left cheek, giving him a new, matching one on the other side. Albert, his machete at the ready, was wrestling with a squat gorilla-shaped man and looked like he was getting the best of him.

We've got a chance! Andy thought as he surveyed the tide of battle. *Phink's men have greater numbers, but it looks like they didn't count on how ferocious the Society members could be in battle.*

That was when Andy suddenly remembered what he was supposed to do. Leaping out from behind the tree where he'd been hiding, he ran down the side of the hill toward the volcano. He hoped the blasts from the professor's cannon had revealed the entrance.

As he ran, Andy reached into his pocket for his Zoomwriter. Suddenly, a pair of black-gloved hands shot out from behind a nearby bush, latching on to his shoulder with a painful grip.

"Aaaah!" Andy shouted. He quickly turned the cap of the pen to the right and, aiming behind his back, pressed down hard.

FOOOM! Like at the Enchanted Tiki room, the atomic pulse blasted backward with tremendous force, tossing his attacker and four others high into the air.

Grateful for his grandfather's gift, Andy continued

his sprint down the side of the hill. The blasted area was just ahead of him. Through the haze of rock dust, he thought he could make out something else there, too.

As he drew closer, what he was seeing became clearer. Beneath the charred and splintered rocks was a small door covered with elaborate carvings. He charged toward the door.

All I have to do is to signal the others when Phink arrives, Andy thought. *Then they'll get the Kapu Key from him. Soon this whole nightmare will be over.*

At last, Andy reached the door. His breath came in ragged gasps as he located a tiny carved hole in its center. He looked from side to side worriedly. What if someone saw him? But the professor was nowhere to be found. He must still have been with his men, attacking the members of the Society. Andy still had time to hide.

Then he heard a voice that sent a chill up his spine. "Thank you, Andy."

Wheeling around, he saw a tall man with uncanny yellow eyes staring down at him. The smile he wore

resembled that of a cat that had just caught an especially clever mouse.

Andy's mind reeled. Hadn't he just seen the professor
about a mile away, standing next to the cannon and
shouting orders? And then, with a sinking feeling, he
realized that the entire thing must have been a distraction. He glanced at the rocks around the opening of the
door and realized that they weren't even hot.

*He used a double to distract us. He's been waiting
for me up here the whole time, planning on taking me by
surprise.*

"You did all this earlier, didn't you?" Andy asked.
"You'd already found the door. The cannon blasts we
saw were a distraction so that you could ambush us and
I would bring you the real Tiki Key."

The professor, as if pleased with one of his students
coming to a correct conclusion, grinned an evil grin.
Andy thought that he'd never seen such a terrible smile
in his life.

"Excellent deductive skills, my boy. Too bad they

won't do you any more good. All the same, so kind of you to bring us the real key . . . Keymaster. Such a shame you won't be collecting any more keys."

Andy was still taking Phink in when he heard another voice.

"We meet again, Andy Stanley."

This time, Andy didn't need to turn to know who it was.

He knew at that moment that his quest was over.

He'd failed.

Chapter Twenty
Last Request

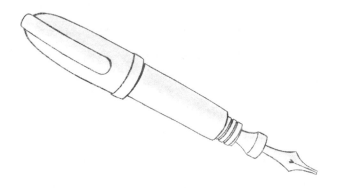

"I have only one question to ask you, Andy Stanley. . . ."

Phink's yellow eyes gleamed as he knelt down beside Andy and continued, "Do you have any last requests? Or shall we dispense with the formalities and get this over with? For you see, once I send you down to the god and you unlock the pendant from Kapu's neck, I can't guarantee what will happen to you. He's been asleep for a thousand years. He might be hungry. . . ."

Stall for time, Andy told himself. *You've got to figure out a way out of this!*

But his mind was blank. It seemed like every thought had been banished by the fear and dread of what he might find when he was sent down the steaming pit that led to the evil Hawaiian god.

This can't be happening!

But it was. And the professor seemed to be thoroughly enjoying Andy's discomfort. Andy was lying facedown on the stone floor, bound head to toe with strong rope. His body was scratched and bruised from his rough treatment, and the sweltering heat inside the volcano was making him lightheaded. Sulfurous fumes wafted from a large pit next to the chamber in which he'd been placed, and Andy couldn't tell if it was the awful stench that was nauseating him, or the terror he felt at the prospect of dying a horrible death.

Andy looked away from Phink. From a shadowy cleft on the other side of the chamber, Abigail Awol watched the situation unfold. Her smile was gone, and Andy thought her expression showed the faintest hint of distaste. Could it be that—now that it had come to this—she was having doubts?

Andy didn't know. But he did know his position was precarious. On the floor next to him was an iron cot. It was connected to a chain that stretched up to the opening of the volcano and looped over a pulley system before dropping back down to the floor.

They're going to put me on that thing and lower me down. Even if this whole thing is a myth and there's no Kapu down there, I'll probably die from the heat of the magma.

His heart raced with panic and he racked his brain for ideas. Professor Phink's question was hanging out there, waiting to be answered. This was his only chance to change his fate. And Phink *did* seem willing to give him a last request.

What should he ask for?

Finally it came to him. He looked up at Abigail,

searching her face for what he hoped to find there. Then, turning his neck painfully so that he could look back into Professor Phink's disturbing gaze, he said, "I do have a last request. . . ."

Phink looked amused. He waved a long-fingered hand as if he were a genie granting a wish. "Ask," he said.

Andy tried to still his thumping heart. Taking a deep breath, he said, "Allow me to write my last will and testament."

Chapter Twenty-One
The Message

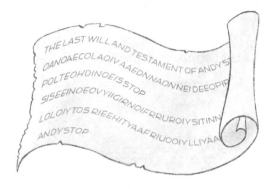

THE LAST WILL AND TESTAMENT OF ANDY S
OANOAECOLAOIV AAEDNNAONNEIDEEOPIR
POLTEOHDINOEISSTOP
SISEEINOEOVYIIGIRNOIERRUROIYSITINN
LOLOIYTOS RIEEHITYAAFRIUOOIYLLIYAA
ANDYSTOP

Ned Lostmore had left for Hawaii just after the zeppelin had gone down and, with the help of Boltonhouse's sophisticated machinery, had remained in contact with the Society throughout Andy's quest.

One of Boltonhouse's many functions was as a submarine. At the moment, he and Ned were traveling underwater at over seventy-five knots. They had already covered nearly two thousand miles from the Oregon coast where Ned's mansion was located and were closing in on Molokai. Ned was safely stowed inside his mechanical servant's chest, protected by waterproof glass, with a wonderful view of the sea life rushing by all around him.

At any another time, the intrepid doctor would have loved looking for shipwrecks or lost continents. But there was no time for that now. He was consumed with worry about his grandson.

Ned had, of course, learned immediately about Phink's attempt to bring down his zeppelin and capture Andy at sea. The realization that his nemesis would resort to such tactics made him furious.

Ned was even more troubled by the fact that Phink and the Collective—the evil organization he worked for—seemed to know as much about the items as he did. He hated to think about the possibility that one of his agents might be a traitor, but *someone* was certainly leaking information to his enemies. The question was, *who*? And how much had this person told the Collective?

As the ocean floor continued to speed by all around him, Ned's troubling thoughts were interrupted by a transmission.

Ned waited impatiently for the slip of paper to scroll into his cabinet.

"Come now! Hurry up! Is it from my grandson?"

Boltonhouse didn't reply. But after a few more seconds of telegraph keys rattling, the paper scroll finally appeared. A tiny claw spread the message out in front of Ned so that he could read what was written there.

THE LAST WILL AND TESTAMENT OF ANDY STANLEY STOP

OANOAECOLAOIV AAEDNNAON NEI DEEOPIPIAORIT STOP

POLTEOH DINOEIS STOP

SISEEINOEOVYIIGIRNOIF RRUROIY SITINNAOW DINMA ULOIY SSEEVROIL LOLOIYTOS RIEEHITYAAF RIUOOIY LLIYAAGGIOBEA STOP

ANDY STOP

Ned's eyes grew wide with surprise. "Increase propeller speed to one hundred knots!" he exclaimed. "And implement Plan 34-X! We must find the menehune!"

Chapter Twenty-Two
The End?

ndy hoped that his gamble had paid off. Having Abigail use the Zoomwriter to write his message had been one of his better ideas. But if it had had any effect, help was slow in coming. He was currently being lowered into the searing pit. Andy could feel the heat of the magma below against his skin.

For now, Andy had no choice but to do as Phink instructed: search for the pendant. Phink had handed him the Kapu Key and ordered him to free the sleeping god—on order of death. He had no intention of unlocking the pendant, but he had to give help a chance to come. Following Phink's orders was the only thing that would buy him time and keep him from getting killed.

Andy's mind raced as he tried to think of a way to thwart the plan. Would there be another tunnel that led out of the volcano when he got to the bottom? If so, maybe he could run for it.

As Andy descended lower and lower into the choking fumes, he blinked back tears at the sulfurous clouds stinging his eyes.

I can hardly see! he thought. *How am I going to find anything down here?* The thought was quickly followed by another. *I don't want to die like this!*

Suddenly, through the smoke, a terrifying sight emerged. Below Andy was a sleeping giant. The prone body of Kapu stretched out on a massive platform of rock. All around it were rivers of magma. Kapu's skin was covered in elaborate tattoos that glowed with a supernatural red light. The tattoos pulsed with each breath the sleeping giant took.

Andy's eyes ran over the giant. He had never seen anything so huge. Kapu had to be over two hundred feet tall! When his eyes reached Kapu's face, Andy's blood ran cold in spite of the terrible heat around him. While the body of the giant resembled that of a human man, the face was something completely different. It was a living tribal mask! Huge almond-shaped eyes gave way to a pair of thin, horribly slitted nostrils. But it was the gigantic mouth that was the worst feature of all. It stretched disproportionately from the god's face like a snout. Inside, Andy could see row after row of razor-sharp teeth. Teeth, if the legend was true, that were made for eating people.

Andy gulped, terrified. He'd never seen anything like Kapu before. *I can't believe it's real! It's like a nightmare!*

Professor Phink's voice echoed down from above. "Do you see it, boy? Do you see it?"

Andy was too stunned to reply. He realized now how stupid his last-ditch effort had been. No one was coming to rescue him. This thing below him was supernatural! A demon! Something far worse than any nightmare he'd ever had!

The iron platform creaked lower, and Andy caught sight of a glint of metal around the giant's neck.

The Pailina Pendant!

"I see it," Andy called. "But I'm not going to touch it. That . . . giant god-thing will kill me!"

A string of curses from above him followed Andy's remark. Andy couldn't help thinking that, had the professor seen what he was seeing, he would have thought twice about his plan. *There's no way that any human could control a creature like this. It looks unstoppable!*

A sharp *CRACK!* echoed through the cavern, followed by a loud *PING!* as a bullet ricocheted just inches from Andy's left hand.

"Hey!" Andy shouted. The professor was shooting at him!

The End?

"Do what I've commanded you to do, boy, or there will be consequences!" Phink shouted.

"Consequences? Do you mean other than being eaten alive by a monster?" Andy shouted back. "If you kill me, who will unlock the pendant?"

The professor cursed again, and Andy felt a jolt. The platform he was riding on shuddered and began to drop!

Andy screamed as the platform free-fell the last twenty-five feet, slamming into the island of stone where Kapu lay with a tremendous *CLANG!*

The boy tumbled from the iron platform—fortunately, Phink had removed his bindings before forcing him onto it—and barely stopped short of slamming into Kapu! He didn't know whether or not the giant could be woken by natural means, but he didn't want to take any chances.

Andy backed away from the god as slowly as possible. A rotten stench emanated from Kapu's mouth. It smelled like rancid meat, and Andy tried to stop himself from thinking about what Kapu's last meal might have been.

Andy's knees were shaking, and as he continued backing up, he forgot to pay attention. He didn't see the loose bit of hardened rock near his heel. And when his foot slipped from beneath him, his only thought was *Don't fall in the magma! Don't fall in the magma!*

For once, Andy's body listened to him. He stopped inches from falling into the sizzling river that flowed on either side of the rocky island.

That was close! Andy thought. His legs shook, but he had a new resolve. *No matter what, even if I have to die, I'll never unlock that pendant. Phink will have to do it himself.*

Just then, Phink's voice called down, "Andy, I have a gun pointed at Abigail's head. If you don't unlock the pendant, Albert Awol's precious daughter will be killed. Do you want that on your conscience?"

Andy gritted his teeth in frustration. He hadn't anticipated Phink using Abigail against him. "Let her go!" he shouted.

Suddenly, a scream rocked the cavern. "Please, n-n-no . . ." Abigail stammered.

What should I do? Andy fretted. *If I don't unlock the pendant, Abigail will die!* He imagined Albert's reaction when he told him that he'd had the chance to save her but hadn't taken it.

Andy looked at the sleeping giant and the pendant that hung around his massive neck.

"If I do this, how do I know that you won't hurt Abigail anyway?" he called up to Phink.

"You don't!" Phink answered. "But are you willing to take that chance?" There was the sound of a gunshot and a sudden cry.

"My leg!" Abigail screamed.

"Abigail!" Andy yelled.

"Now then, that little demonstration should convince you that I'm serious about killing her," said Phink. "Next time, I won't be aiming low. You have three seconds to make your decision, Andy Stanley." He began to count. "Three . . . two . . ."

Andy couldn't let Abigail die. He reached into his pocket and removed the Kapu Key.

"All right, Phink. You win! I'll do it," Andy called. "Let her go!"

There was the sound of a scuffle far above. Andy hoped it meant that Phink had released his grip on Abigail.

"Make it quick, Andy! I'm running out of patience!" Phink called.

Andy examined the key. Unlike the Tiki Key, this one was metal. Its surface was rough and pitted, and the handle was unadorned. If he'd stumbled upon this key anywhere else, he would have thought it just a simple door key.

Maybe that's why it's been secret for so long. Nobody would expect that a little thing like this was capable of releasing a monster.

As if in a dream, Andy walked to the sleeping giant. He felt completely numb, like what he was doing was too much for his mind to comprehend.

The End?

Andy took a deep breath. *Here we go....*

He winced as he turned the key in the lock. There was a sharp click. And then, the Pailina Pendant fell from the giant's neck, dragging a thin iron chain behind it.

Kapu's giant eyelids fluttered open, revealing glowing red eyeballs.

This is bad, Andy thought as he backed away. *This is really, really bad!*

With a rumble that shook the walls of the volcano, the giant rose from where he'd been sleeping and let out a tremendous roar.

Rocks showered down around Andy, and a particularly large boulder slammed into the rocky floor.

Fortunately, Kapu was so intent upon leaving his prison that he took no notice of Andy. The god was rising to his feet. Rising from the pit.

The delicate spell that had held him captive was broken.

—

Professor Phink stood at the rim of the pit, staring down into the murky haze below. He raised his gun, preparing to shoot down at the boy again.

Perhaps it was because Abigail sensed what the professor meant to do. Or perhaps it was because, after hearing the supernatural roar of Kapu, she knew that things had gone too far. Either way, something in her snapped. In spite of her injured leg, she mustered her strength and slammed into the professor with all her might. But Abigail was not strong enough to push him over the edge. Instead, the impact jarred Phink, and his finger pushed on the trigger of the gun. The bullet ricocheted off the cavern walls.

Phink turned, fury blazing in his yellow eyes. "That was a mistake," he growled.

Looking at the man, Abigail was reminded that he was much more physically formidable than she. She started to back away, but the cavern was small, and Abigail soon found herself backed against a wall.

Phink stalked toward her, an expression on his face

unlike any Abigail had ever seen before. She steeled herself for an attack. But it never came. Instead, a gigantic tattooed hand grabbed the professor from behind. The man screamed in surprise as he was lifted high into the air!

Abigail's eyes grew wide as she saw the monstrous head emerge from the pit.

Kapu was awake, and he was hungry!

"Put me down!" Phink screamed. "I command you to put me down!"

But it didn't work. Kapu wasn't listening. The panicked Professor Phink yelled once more, trying in his most authoritative voice to command the god to release him. He wriggled his hand free and shot his pistol directly at the evil god, but the bullets bounced harmlessly from his stony body.

Kapu raised the professor toward his rows of razor-sharp teeth, howling with hunger and fury.

Seconds later, Phink was gone. All that remained of the villain was a single black glove that fluttered down,

down, down into the steaming crack in the earth below.

Abigail ducked behind a large stone outcropping as the giant climbed to the surface of the pit and, with a tremendous roar, shot through the top of the volcano like an eruption.

The echo of Kapu's cry died away and was replaced by an eerie silence. From somewhere far below, a boy's thin and frightened voice shouted, "Can someone please get me out of here?"

Chapter Twenty-Three

Rescue

Andy stood face-to-face with the young woman who'd nearly killed him. Neither one knew what to say.

"Are you okay?" Andy asked, gazing with concern at the blood that stained her trouser leg.

Abigail winced and nodded. "The bullet grazed me, but I'm all right." She gave Andy a wry smile. "That last will and testament idea was pretty good. It was easy to decipher the code you sent."

Andy grinned. "I thought you might figure it out."

She nodded. "I've been trained in all of the Society's secret codes and languages. My father was grooming me to be a member. . . ." Her voice trailed off at the mention of her father, and she gazed thoughtfully at the floor.

Andy shifted uncomfortably, unsure what to say.

"If what you said was true," she said quietly, "about him still loving me and wanting my forgiveness, I . . . well . . . I mean, there's nothing I'd rather . . ."

"You don't have to say it," Andy told her, finding his voice. "I know you and your father had a difficult relationship after your mother died. . . ."

Abigail looked up sharply. "He told you about that?"

Andy nodded.

Abigail flushed with embarrassment. "I was upset. I needed someone to blame for what had happened, and . . . I guess I didn't know where to put my anger."

Andy was startled to see tears forming in Abigail's eyes. "I knew deep down that working for the Collective was wrong. But I just couldn't let go of my anger toward my father. Your letter reminded me of how much I've lost. I guess I've known it for a long time, but didn't want to think about it."

They were both quiet for a long moment. Andy could see that talking about the old wounds she'd nursed for so long was tough for Abigail, but it seemed she wanted to talk to someone about how she felt.

"I should have known better than to trust the professor," Abigail continued, wiping her eyes. "And when I saw that he actually would have killed me back there, it only made things clearer. My father was right about him. I should have listened."

Abigail glanced at the spot where Kapu had appeared moments before. Her gaze hardened. "He got exactly what he deserved. You know, up until that thing came out of the volcano, I thought this whole search for the pendant and the key was no more than an eccentric superstition."

Abigail turned her gaze back to Andy. Her lips were pressed tight in a determined expression. "I want to make things right," she said. "What can I do?"

"You really want to help?" Andy asked.

Abigail nodded. "I do. It's the only way I can make up for the mistakes I've made. Do you think the Society will allow me to make amends?"

Andy grew thoughtful. "Honestly, I'm not sure. I'm new to this whole thing myself." He gave Abigail a small smile. "But I'll vouch for you and tell them how you helped me back there. Maybe having Ned Lostmore's grandson on your side will count for something."

Abigail offered a contrite smile. "Thanks for rescuing me. Phink really would have killed me—I know that for sure now. What you did took a lot of courage."

Andy smiled back. "I know you tried to stop him—to save me. Consider us even," he said, extending his hand. Abigail smiled and shook it. An awkward pause descended between the two of them.

Finally, Abigail broke the silence.

"We've got to hurry if we're going to stop that thing," she said.

"But what about the pendant?" Andy asked. "It's still down there."

Abigail gazed back down into the pit where Kapu had been sleeping just moments before.

"I'll go back down there and get it. If it put him to sleep once before, my guess is that it will do it again. We just need to find the spell to lock it around his neck," Abigail said.

Andy nodded solemnly. "Madame Wiki will know what to do!"

Andy and Abigail ran from the cave. When they got to the clearing where the others were, they were surprised to see that the rest of Phink's mercenaries had gone. Rusty, breathing hard from the recent battle, indicated the many fallen enemies that surrounded them.

"The rest ran like cowards," Betty said grimly. Andy noticed that she was busy tending to a wound on her sister's arm, winding it with bandages.

"Listen, I need to tell you something," Andy said. He

gestured to where Abigail was standing a little away from the group, fidgeting nervously and staring at her feet.

"I wondered when you'd be getting to that," Rusty said coldly.

"She saved my life and turned her back on Phink," Andy explained. "I would have never escaped if it hadn't been for her. I really think she wants to make amends and help fix all this."

Cedric spoke up, giving Abigail a wary glance. "How do we know we can trust her? What if this is an elaborate ruse by Phink to gain our trust and betray our secrets?"

Andy folded his arms. "There's more. Professor Phink is dead. Kapu woke up and ate him. Which means we have bigger problems. Abigail went back into that pit to get the pendant back. I give my word as Ned Lostmore's grandson that I believe her when she says that she's changed. She wants to help defeat Kapu."

Andy gazed around the group with a defiant expression. "Does anyone want to challenge me on that?"

The group fell silent. Then Rusty Bucketts grinned and smacked Andy so hard on the back that he thought he might have dislocated something.

"HA! That's the spirit, boy! Sounds just like his old grandfather, doesn't he?"

Andy smiled and was relieved to see that the others were smiling, too.

The twins tilted their heads in unison, studying Abigail for a long moment. Finally, Dotty spoke up. "She could be dangerous. But for Albert's sake, I think we should do it. If there's any chance at healing the rift between them, we should try."

At the mention of his name, Andy realized Albert was missing. "Wait a minute. Where is he?" he asked.

The others exchanged puzzled glances. "He and Hoku were fighting just over the ridge. I haven't seen either of them since the battle ended," Rusty said.

Andy glanced over at Abigail. He knew she had been looking forward to making peace with her father. It seemed that would have to wait. Andy hoped that wherever Albert was, he was okay. But with Kapu on the loose, he couldn't spend too much time worrying about one missing friend.

The boat ride back to the base camp was subdued. The nervous energy they'd felt on the way to the island had been replaced by fear. They had a big job to do, and none of them was sure they were up to it.

When they arrived at the docks, they found Madame Wiki waiting for them. She'd seen the top of Nanea explode when Kapu flew out of the volcano, and she'd suspected that something had gone wrong with the plan. One look at their faces confirmed her fears.

"It seems we have a problem," she said with a grim smile.

Just seeing her, Andy felt a wave of relief.

She'll know what to do.

"Do you know how to make the magic work to put Kapu back in his prison?" Andy asked when he had explained what happened. "We have the pendant. . . ."

Madame Wiki stared at the pendant in his outstretched hand. For the first time since Andy had met her, she looked like she didn't have an answer.

The old medicine woman shook her head slowly. "This kind of magic is very ancient and powerful. It is kept by the spirits of the islands. We mortals don't know its secrets!"

"But if the legends are true, then Kapu will destroy the world!" said Betty. "We won't be able to stop him!"

Dotty nodded in agreement.

"Where do you think Kapu has gone?" Abigail asked.

Madame Wiki turned to Abigail, her face grim. "There's only one possible place that Kapu could be," she said. Her expression darkened and her voice grew quiet. "The legends say that when he's released upon the world, his hunger will know no bounds. He will go where he can find the most people."

Andy thought about the geography of Hawaii. As far as he could remember, Molokai, the little island they were on, was largely uninhabited. But there was another island nearby.

"You don't mean . . . ?" he began.

Madame Wiki nodded.

The others exchanged confused glances. Abigail was the first to understand. "Oh, no," she said, turning pale. Then, turning to Rusty, she said, "We're gonna need that boat!"

Chapter Twenty-Four
Honolulu

The gentle sounds of tropical music lulled Mrs. Peggy Benson into a light doze. Her chubby, sunburned legs were slathered with a generous amount of sunscreen, and she was sipping a tropical drink from a hollowed pineapple.

Her trip to Honolulu had been an impulsive decision. Everyone at the bank where she worked in Toledo, Ohio, had been green with envy when she had announced that she'd be taking all the vacation days that she'd managed to save up over the last fifteen years of employment.

She'd relished the looks on their faces—especially Gertrude Butts's. Peggy and Gertrude had hated each other for years, and that dislike had only been aggravated by the fact that their desks were right next to each other.

The ground beneath Peggy's painted toenails shook. She glanced at her pineapple, noticing that the drink had sloshed over the side.

Peggy stared at the frozen concoction for a moment and then called out in a shrill voice, "Waiter! I'm going to need another . . ."

She'd been about to say "drink," but the word turned into a scream of panic as a horrifying monster, larger even than the hotel in which she was staying, reached into the swimming pool and grabbed a handful of swimmers.

Kapu chomped delightedly, obviously relishing the cries of his victims as he grabbed at the crowd of sunburned humans.

—

Andy and the members of the Jungle Explorers' Society came ashore at a sandy cove near Waikiki Beach.

As Andy stepped out of the boat, he noticed that Abigail wasn't moving. "Are you okay?" he asked.

"Actually, no," she confessed.

"What's wrong?"

Abigail hesitated. "I'm worried about my father. No one has seen him. For all we know, he's still on the island with a volcano that could erupt any minute. And now we're supposed to face off against this horrible monster that I'm responsible for waking. And if we can't stop him, he'll destroy the world. And it will be my fault. And . . . I'm scared."

Andy nodded. "I'm scared, too. But Albert is a member of the Society. He knows how to take care of himself. And they'd never let him stay lost. For now, we need to stop Kapu. If you want to prove to the Society that you've changed, helping now is the best way to do it."

Abigail nodded. Andy could tell by her resolute expression that she intended to follow his suggestion.

Andy offered Abigail his hand. Holding it tightly, she stepped out of the boat. The two took in the evidence of Kapu's destruction. Roofs were smashed and debris was everywhere.

It's even worse than I thought it would be, Andy thought. *It looks like an entire army came through here.*

The others must have been feeling the same way. Every member of the Society wore the same hopeless expression.

Then Andy had an idea. Wasn't his pen meant to summon help? Why hadn't he thought of it before? His grandfather seemed to know all about magic and curses. He might have an answer!

Andy removed the pen from his pocket. Its jade barrel gleamed in the afternoon sun. Placing the cap on the back of the pen, Andy turned to the others. "My grandfather said that if I press down three times on the cap, help will come. I'm not altogether certain what form it will take, but seeing as it helped me once before when I nearly drowned . . ."

The others crowded around to watch. Andy took a deep breath. He was about to press down on the cap when a familiar voice interrupted, stopping him short.

"That won't be necessary. I'm already one step *ahead* of you. Ha! Good one, what? A-*head* of you?"

As one, the group wheeled around. On the beach behind them stood Boltonhouse. Andy noticed that his grandfather's mechanical servant had huge motors equipped with futuristic-looking propellers strapped to his back. But it was what was in the center of the robot's body that held Andy's attention. The door to Boltonhouse's chest had been replaced by a thick sheet of glass. Bobbing merrily inside was Ned Lostmore.

"I set out after the zeppelin went down," explained Ned. "Boltonhouse is equipped with the fastest underwater engines ever made. It also helped that we found a rather speedy current that was headed in this direction. Modern science, don't you know!"

Cheers erupted from the group. Most hadn't seen Ned since the incident at the hidden temple.

When the excited chatter died down, Ned told the group that he had a plan. Andy breathed a sigh of relief. *I knew we could count on him.*

Chapter Twenty-Five
The Menehune

"**W**e need to find the menehune," Ned said. "They know the deepest magic in the islands. If anyone knows how to activate the spell that will allow us to lock the pendant back around Kapu's neck, it is they."

Madame Wiki nodded. "I should have thought of it before. To enslave a god requires powerful magic. The menehune will know the spell—if we can convince them to help."

Andy tried to focus and block out the screams of the tourists that seemed to emanate from everywhere around them. He knew that time was short if they hoped to save the remaining population from the horror that was making its way through the city.

"How do we find them?" he asked.

Madame Wiki smiled. "It's quite easy, if you just know where to look. The menehune have called the Iolani Palace home for a generation."

Andy and the others arrived at the Iolani Palace to find the gates open and the grounds empty.

"We must hurry," Ned said. "Boltonhouse, the banana, if you please."

Andy stopped short and turned to his grandfather. "Wait. Did you say 'banana'?"

"Of course!" Ned said, bobbing away behind the glass in Boltonhouse's chest. "The menehune love them. It's the only way to get one to come out into the open. Did you know, by the way, that a banana is also a wonderful cure for the Nairobi rooster pox when smeared beneath the armpits? Now come on, no time to waste!"

Andy chuckled. *I really should be terrified right now, but I'm not. I don't know if it's because Grandfather is here or if it's something else, but it actually feels like we might get through this.*

Something inside Andy had grown since he'd started his adventure. He had learned what real fear was, and he knew that it would come and go. But he had also learned that true bravery wasn't about feeling no fear. It was deciding to press on in spite of it.

Andy felt oddly at peace with himself as they raced up the gleaming white stairs and into the palace that had once housed Hawaii's king and queen. If the danger hadn't been so pressing, Andy would have loved to look around at the palace's grand halls and magnificent portraits, but now was not the time.

At Ned's command, the group halted in front of a small fountain at the end of a side corridor. A tiny brass plate sat next to the fountain, so small it would go completely unnoticed if one did not know what to look for.

Andy read the tiny words engraved on the plate: HERE LIVES ALIKA, THE ROYAL MENEHUNE.

Andy looked around. He didn't see any kind of dwelling. The fountain in front of them looked ordinary enough and was filled with glittering pennies and dimes, wishes made by fun-loving tourists.

"Cedric, the banana, if you please?" Ned said.

The witch doctor took the yellow fruit from Boltonhouse and held it over the fountain. The air around it began to shimmer. Suddenly, a little man with a long white mustache appeared in front of them.

Incredible! Andy thought. He grinned at the merry little figure in front of him. *At least he looks friendly.*

"Aloha!" the menehune said in a cheery voice. Then he noticed the banana. His eyes grew wide and he licked his lips. "A *mai'a!*" he said happily.

The menehune looked around at the group who had summoned him. When he saw Ned, the smile immediately disappeared from his face. "Your head is much smaller than when I saw you last. You have been affected by bad magic."

Ned, whose head was about the size of Alika's own, bobbed up and down. He flashed the tiny man a big smile and his blue eyes glittered. "Indeed, you speak true," he said.

The menehune narrowed his eyes. "What is it you want from me this time, Ned Lostmore? We agreed that you'd already had the help of my people and that you would never return. We do not have the power to undo this magic."

"O great Alika," Ned began. "I wouldn't bother you at all, except that your land is in danger. The evil god Kapu has been awoken from his sleep, and we must have your help."

Alika's eyes grew wide and his face serious. The menehune had obviously not expected this. "Do you have the Pailina Pendant?" he asked.

Ned nodded to Andy, who removed it from his

pocket and handed it to the tiny man. Alika stared at it, turning it over and nodding his head.

"I can recite the spell to activate it, but in order to subdue Kapu, you must ask for Kane's aid. This, of course, is very dangerous. Very dangerous indeed."

Andy noticed that while he was speaking, the menehune had taken the banana from Cedric and placed it in a small woven pouch of palm leaves at his belt. He placed the pendant on the floor and motioned for everyone to step back. Then, closing his eyes, he began to chant.

Andy's eyes grew wide as a magical glow surrounded the pendant. The magic here was even stronger than the kind that Madame Wiki had performed in the Tiki Room. There was something about it that reminded Andy of the earth, and of the Hawaiian breezes and warm rain. It seemed to have a smell, too, like hibiscus flowers warmed by the afternoon sun.

The menehune lifted the glowing pendant and handed it back to Andy. "The only way to summon Kane is to touch Kapu with the pendant. You must call out for Kane to come to your aid and subdue his brother. But listen well, boy. You must be very careful. If you aren't . . ."

The menehune stared up at Andy with a serious expression. Andy didn't need him to go on. He knew what the rest of the sentence was.

"He'll eat me up," Andy finished.

Chapter Twenty-Six
His Bravest Moment

The group piled into an abandoned car and Rusty drove them in the direction of the loudest screams. When they arrived at the devastating scene, they were amazed anew at the level of destruction that Kapu had already caused.

Countless cars had been thrown into the sides of buildings. Andy saw a black Studebaker sticking out of the side of a hotel balcony, its hazard lights still flashing.

People were screaming, trying to avoid Kapu's grasp. The giant howled with frustration as the people hid in hard-to-reach areas, even resorting to climbing inside metal trash bins.

"If he gets too close, I want you to use this," Andy said, handing his Zoomwriter to Abigail. "Turn the cap to the right and press the top."

Abigail's eyes grew wide. "An A.P.E. gun? How in the world did you get it?"

Andy grinned. "It was a present from my grandfather," he said, winking at Ned.

Abigail tried to hand the pen back to Andy. "I can't take this. You might need it. You won't have a weapon. . . ."

Andy gently pushed her hand back. "I'm fine. If . . . well . . . if something happens to me, I want you to have it. You saved my life back at the volcano."

Abigail flashed him a smile. "You're a very brave boy, did you know that?"

Andy flushed with pleasure. And because he didn't

know what to say, he opened the car door and prepared to jump.

The others piled out after him, determined to distract the god while Andy moved close.

"Hey, big shot!" Rusty called. The bush pilot waved his hands over his head. "Over here!"

The giant must have had exceptional hearing, for he spotted Rusty right away. Dropping an uprooted palm tree, Kapu let out a tremendous earsplitting roar.

"Everyone spread out!" Ned commanded.

The group obeyed. Following Rusty's lead, they shouted and tried to distract Kapu.

The god was unprepared for such a display and began randomly grasping for the group. But he soon found that these were not like the scared tourists he'd been feasting upon. This prey was far more crafty and agile!

As Kapu grabbed for Boltonhouse, the robot rocketed out of his grasp. Kapu's fist slammed into the street where Ned and his mechanical servant had been a split second before.

When Kapu grabbed at the twins, they reacted just as quickly, tumbling through the air like expert gymnasts and landing safely in a hotel canopy.

But the biggest surprise was Molly the mime, who didn't move at all. She simply stood in place, juggling.

Andy saw from where he was hiding that she was good.

Incredibly good!

The balls flew upward to impossible heights. The higher they went, it seemed, the more there were. For once, the mime wasn't talking. Instead, she was centered in concentration, juggling with practiced expertise.

"Blimey," Cedric said. "I didn't know she could do that."

Kapu froze in place, staring at the dancing balls with an almost hypnotized expression.

Andy knew this was his chance. He leapt from the cover of the trees, racing as fast as he could toward Kapu's gigantic feet. He hurtled over a fallen palm tree and neatly dodged two gigantic potholes where the giant's fists had broken the pavement.

Andy was focused on what he had to do. The distance between him and the giant shortened as he ran faster and faster. His heart swelled with confidence and courage!

But the sudden movement caught Kapu's eye and broke the spell. Tearing his eyes away from the juggling balls, he reached for the boy.

"Stay away from him!" Abigail shouted. An atomic pulse shot from the pen in her outstretched hand, its force slamming into Kapu's left leg.

The weapon had little effect on the supernatural being, but it did capture his attention. With a movement quicker than anyone would have thought possible for a creature so huge, Kapu grabbed Abigail and raised her to his gaping mouth.

Abigail screamed! Andy stared upward, helpless to do anything.

Just then a voice sounded behind Andy. This one stopped Kapu in his tracks.

"That's my daughter!" Albert bellowed.

Andy didn't know when he'd arrived on the scene, but the grizzled boat captain ran at the god full speed, a machete in each hand.

"Look at me, you ugly excuse for a tiki!"

The giant swung his head to look at Albert. His eyes widened at the sight of the weapons.

"What are you doing?" Andy yelled.

"A witch doctor gave me these!" Albert shouted back over his shoulder. "They're magically cursed!"

Albert slammed into the giant and plunged the machetes to the hilts into Kapu's big toe. The god let out a howl of rage as the machetes' magic coursed through his body.

"YES!" Andy shouted.

It can actually feel pain! We may be able to stop him yet!

The magic was indeed strong. It was not enough to destroy Kapu, but it was certainly enough to hurt him!

Then something terrible happened. The howling

giant dropped Abigail, who plunged toward the street below.

I'm not close enough! Andy thought, panicked. *I can't help her!*

But Albert hadn't taken his eyes off his daughter for a single second. He was beneath her in an instant and caught her neatly. As they both tumbled to the ground, Andy realized with a surge of relief that she would be okay.

The boy looked up at the angry Kapu. His eyes burned with determination. Kapu had to be stopped. Andy would do whatever it took to bring him down. This had gone on long enough!

Taking advantage of the fact that the giant was distracted by the pain in his toe, Andy leapt onto Kapu's ankle. As he clutched the monster's giant foot, hanging on for dear life, he removed the pendant from his pocket.

Steady! he told himself. *Don't fall!*

Andy pressed the pendant against the monster's

tattooed flesh. Then, following the menehune's advice, he yelled, "Kane!"

A mighty kick sent Andy tumbling into a nearby bank of sand. Andy slammed into it but hardly felt the impact. *I did it!* he thought. *I really did it!*

Suddenly, the sky dimmed and the wind began to blow. As if a switch had been turned off, Kapu forgot his pain and turned in the direction of the wind, his glowing red eyes narrowing with hate.

The breeze became a howling gale, blowing sand everywhere and forcing Andy to shield his eyes. Through the swirling sand came a form, a giant as big as Kapu but more humanlike in appearance. His eyes flicked down to Andy, who held up the pendant.

Two fingers took the magic pendant gently from Andy's hand. And then, with a quick smile at Andy, the giant turned to face his evil brother.

Kane had returned!

Chapter Twenty-Seven
Brother vs. Brother

At the sight of his brother, Kapu roared! Spittle flew from his mouth and he leapt toward Kane, fists raised, ready to attack.

Andy and his friends ran for cover. "Quick, over there!" Rusty shouted, pointing to a fallen palm tree. The group huddled behind the massive trunk and watched the titanic battle unfold.

It's like a Greek myth, Andy thought, feeling awe-struck. *Two gods who hate each other engaged in an epic struggle.*

Kapu lifted a car above his head and threw it at his brother, howling with frustration and anger. Kane ducked at the last possible moment. The car flew over his head and smashed into a row of park benches by the beach, shattering them in a shower of splintered wood and metal.

"I think Kane has underestimated him," Albert growled. "His brother has been imprisoned for over a thousand years and seems to carry a grudge."

"Get him, Kane!" shouted Molly. "Give him the old one-two!"

Kane rushed at his brother. He slammed into Kapu's chest, tackling him to the ground.

The earth shook from the impact of Kane hitting the ground, and Andy was knocked backward.

"Oh, no!" Abigail shouted. "Look!"

Kane may have had the advantage when he'd taken

Kapu down, but the evil god had responded by sinking his razor-sharp teeth deep into his brother's shoulder. The god let out a cry of pain as the fangs penetrated his flesh.

"We need to do something!" Andy cried.

"We can't," Ned said. "This is between them. Only Kane can stop him now."

Kane wrested himself from his brother's jaws and—with a mighty shove—pushed him backward. The giant crashed into the wall of a large apartment building. Debris showered down upon Kapu, who seemed dazed from the force of the collision.

"NOW!" Andy shouted. His fists were clenched, turning his knuckles white.

Whether Kane heard Andy or not, nobody knew. But the giant seemed to sense his advantage. He leapt at his brother and put him in a fierce choke hold.

With his free hand, Kane wrapped the Pailina Pendant around his brother's neck. There was an audible crack as the pendant locked.

As quickly as it had started, the battle was over. Kane raised his noble head to the sky and let out a victorious shout. The two gigantic figures shimmered and slowly faded from view, until all that remained was the echo of Kane's voice merging with the thunderous surf and becoming one with the sounds of the mighty ocean.

Kapu was imprisoned once more.

Chapter Twenty-Eight
Aftermath

That night, the Society held a luau at Albert's house, down on the beach next to his trusty boat, *Amazon Annie.*

There were plates filled with delicious food—plenty of fresh fruit and fish, and a Hawaiian dish called laulau that was specially prepared by Madame Wiki. Andy wasn't sure, but he thought that she must have used some of her island magic to make it, because it was by far the best meal he'd ever tasted.

A warm glow filled Andy's chest as he watched Albert and Abigail walk down the beach, chatting with each other. They had much to catch up on after being apart for so long.

The rest of Jungle Explorers' Society sat at a table, each trying to outdo the next with tales of daring and adventure. Even Hoku was chattering away, excited to be reunited with a very happy Albert and Abigail.

"So how did you like your first adventure? Thrilling, eh?" Ned asked.

Andy turned to look at his grandfather. Somehow, someone had managed to get a small cup of pineapple juice into Boltonhouse's chest compartment, allowing the old man to enjoy the festivities with the others.

Andy didn't know whether his grandfather needed to eat or drink and didn't want to ask. Instead, he decided to answer the question. "I can hardly believe it's over," he said. He was surprised to hear a hint of sadness in his voice. "Kapu is inside the volcano again, sleeping like before, and Phink is gone."

Ned chuckled. "And most importantly, the Tiki Key and the Kapu Key are now safe. As Keymaster, you must make sure that our enemies never get them back. Remember, the Collective is filled with villains. Now that they know who you are, they will come for you again."

Ned noticed his grandson's somber expression and said, "My dear boy, you mustn't feel down. Would you like me to prescribe you a happiness tonic made from Norwegian slugs? I daresay that it would perk you up!"

Andy sighed and looked out over the water. The moon was huge. It cast a beautiful reflection on the gently rolling sea.

"I just don't want this to be over," he admitted. "I don't want to go back to being who I was before—scared of everything."

Andy glanced over at his smiling grandfather, noting how his grin lifted his white whiskers high up on his ruddy cheeks. His monocle glinted and his blue eyes sparkled.

"My dear boy, don't you know that adventures are

never over? There's always one waiting for you if you have the courage to look for it."

Andy smiled at his grandfather. "Thank you for everything. Especially for believing in me."

Ned smiled kindly. "You, my boy, are indeed a Lostmore through and through. I knew from the beginning what you were capable of, even if you didn't. Reading about adventures is one thing. But living them, well, that's quite another.

"Now," Ned said, "it seems we have another adventure waiting for us. There's a little something called the Golden Paw . . . an item that gives its owner great and terrible powers. I could use your help to make sure our enemies don't get to it first. It would be another chance to prove your worth to the Society."

Andy's grin widened and he glanced down at his chest pocket. The medal he'd been given was still there.

The Silver Sacroiliac.

He felt in his pocket for his pen. The Hodges Zoomwriter was still there, too.

Ned noticed and said, "Well, Keymaster. How would you feel about going on another adventure?"

Andy remembered being asked this question once before. At that time, he hadn't known what to say.

He puffed out his chest. This time he knew the right answer to that question. He knew what everyone should say when asked if they're up for a new adventure.

"Absolutely."